Rebecca Barrett

Callahan's Savannah Caper

Secret Staircase Books

Rebecca Barrett

Callahan's Savannah Caper

Cat Callahan Mysteries, Book 3

Secret Staircase Books

Callahan's Savannah Caper
Published by Secret Staircase Books, an imprint of
Columbine Publishing Group LLC
PO Box 416, Angel Fire, NM 87710

Book layout and design by Secret Staircase Books
Illustrations by Becky's Graphic Design, Oxilixo, Sean Pavone,
BooksRme, Veremer
First e-book edition: February, 2024
First paperback edition: February, 2024

Publisher's Cataloging-in-Publication Data

Barrett, Rebecca
Callahan's Savannah Caper / by Rebecca Barrett.
p. cm.
ISBN 978-1649141699 (paperback)
ISBN 978-1649141705 (e-book)

1. Cat Callahan (Fictitious character)—Fiction. 2. Mystery—
Fiction. 3. Amateur sleuths—Fiction. 4. Animals in mystery fiction.
I. Title

Cat Callahan Mystery Series, Book 3.
Barrett, Rebecca, Cat Callahan Cozy Mysteries.

BISAC : FICTION / Mystery.

813/.54

For CeCe and Binnie, champions of all living creatures, especially cats. Never mind that CeCe claims to be a dog person. We know where her heart is.

Chapter One

I open my eyes wide, then narrow them to mere slits. My ears perk up and my tail twitches. I rise from the cushion of the window seat and peer out into the shadows, my superior feline senses at full alert. A sound has disturbed me from that light sleep of the born hunter.

My tail twitches back and forth with anticipation. Here at last is something to relieve the boredom of our stopover in sleepy Savannah, Georgia, something to pique my curiosity and engage my sleuthing skills. Some dirt bag is attempting to rob the office of my sleeping companion of the moment.

A muffled thud sounds from below and I'm off the window seat in a flash. The noise is coming from the ground floor, from the office of The Hampton Detective Agency. I slide across the hardwood floor to a halt at the apartment door. It's closed and probably locked. It's a solid, old door in a solid, old house on Calhoun Square.

I turn almost before I reach the door and retrace my steps with a couple of springs of my powerful hind legs. The window is open six inches, just enough room for me to slip through, catwalk the molding of the building, drop to the awning, and then to the ground. But that won't do me any good. Those noises came from inside the office below.

In less than twenty seconds from the first thump that woke me, I decide the only course of action is to involve my current roommate, Julia.

Without a second thought I spring onto the bed that dominates the room, walk onto Julia's chest, and sit. I bat at her face with my paw. Stealth is the only weapon we have at the moment before the nature of the not-so-secretive activity below is known.

Julia rises from her prone position and a deep sleep in one swift move. I slip from her chest.

"What? What?"

She isn't fully awake. I reach my paw up to her lips in an effort to silence her.

Julia brushes her hair back from her face and reaches for me.

"Callahan? What's the matter?" *She yawns.* "You want to go out?"

Again, I place a paw over her lips then jump from the bed and head for the door. Another muffled thud comes from below.

Julia sits up straight, suddenly alert. She whispers, "What's that?" *as she eases out of the bed and follows barefoot after me.*

She presses her ear against the heavy apartment door and listens. I bat at the door with my paws and growl low in my throat.

Julia retrieves a long, heavy-duty flashlight from a drawer in the bombe chest next to the entry. She carefully turns the deadbolt lock so as not to make a sound, then places her finger to her lips. "Shhhhh." *The door swings open on silent hinges.*

The noise downstairs is louder now, drawers opening and closing, paper shuffled. It's evident someone is ransacking Julia's desk and file cabinet. I race ahead, taking the stairs as silently as a panther stalking his prey. In an instant, I'm out of Julia's sight and have picked my way across the shattered glass from the French doors that are the entrance from the foyer into the detective agency's office.

Two thugs are hard at it, one searching through the files in the file cabinet and dumping folders unceremoniously onto the floor, while the other is at her desk trying to access her computer records.

I make my way unnoticed under the desk as the crunch of glass beneath Julia's bare feet alerts the intruders that they've been discovered. Both men look up and the one at the desk immediately kills the lamp light. I spring at him and catch his leg in my claws. By this time both men are headed for the door. Julia thinks to turn on the flashlight just as both of them barrel into her, knocking her to the glass-littered floor. I'm unable to hang on to the perp's pants leg but I dig my claws into his calf, extracting a muttered curse before he shakes free of my grip. As they slip out into the night, all I have left is a scrap of fabric.

Torn between the chase and the fallen Julia, I reluctantly give in to my new-found sense of responsibility for humans and go to her aid.

* * *

Sergeant Gibbons arrived on the scene within minutes of Julia's call to 911. He pushed his hat onto the back of his head and sighed. "Your father isn't going to like this, Julia."

"Do you have to tell him?"

"It wouldn't be right if I didn't."

Julia bit back the response that was on the tip of her tongue. She hadn't lived at home since her return to Savannah after college but that hadn't prevented her father from keeping a watchful eye over her. At twenty-eight she was more than an adult, more than capable of taking care of herself, but she knew she'd always, in her father's eyes, be daddy's little girl. And all the cops who patrol the historic district of Savannah knew it too. Sometimes her father's social standing and political influence were maddening.

Julia lifted her hands in a gesture of surrender. "Fine. But don't make it sound worse than it is."

Sergeant Gibbons looked about at the mess in her office and the broken pane of glass in the French door. Finally, his gaze came to rest on her arm. "But you're bleeding."

"You would be too if you walked barefoot in the dark over broken glass."

"What about your arm? How did that happen?"

Julia looked away from Sergeant Gibbons and surveyed the disaster in her office. "I cut it on the door."

He glanced down at his notepad. "So, there were two of them, both wearing ski masks, about five-ten to six feet tall."

"Yes."

"And you can't say what they were after?"

"I can't say because I don't know. As far as I can tell they were searching for something in my files. I won't know until I sort through this mess."

He slapped the notebook closed. "So, there was nothing distinctive about either of them that you remember?"

Julia lifted her shoulders in a faint shrug. "I only saw them for less than a minute. When I stepped on the broken glass, the one at my desk turned off the lamp."

"Well, we'll dust for prints but I doubt we find any. Crooks these days know how to cover their tracks. Too many cop shows on TV."

He was about to turn into the office when he spotted Callahan sitting on the third step of the stairs. "I didn't know you had a cat."

"I don't. I'm taking him to the vet tomorrow for a friend."

Callahan raised his hackles and growled low in his throat.

"Not very friendly, is he?"

Julia laughed. "Callahan is a free spirit. He isn't pleased at being confined in my apartment for the next few days."

With that Callahan turned his back on the two of them and began to groom himself.

Julia laughed again. "As you can see."

After Sergeant Gibbons finally left, taking the young policeman who spent more time ogling her than collecting evidence, Julia surveyed the mess in her office. What could the two men have been searching for? Except for a discreet plaque with gold lettering beside the outer door of the building there was no way of knowing this house was any different from all the other mostly residential houses on the square. This wasn't a random break-in. They were looking for something specific, something in her files.

She thought back over the past few weeks and months. All her cases were in the end stages of resolution. The information from her research had been reported to the insurance company that employed her, the conclusions already on file. She had a court hearing in two weeks on one of them and an arbitration hearing scheduled next month on another. A lot of money was at stake in the arbitration case but not so much on the court case. How would her files benefit either of them?

Well, there was no way to know until she established some sense of order.

As soon as the policemen left the premises, Callahan began a circuitous inspection of the room. He pawed a couple of manila folders on the floor, sniffed the drawer pull on the file cabinet, but quickly moved on. The desk chair piqued his interest. He placed his nose to the seat of the chair and sneezed. Next, he inspected several items on the desktop: a stapler, a letter opener, the lamp, and finally the keyboard of the computer. He sat squarely in the middle of the desk blotter and blinked slowly three times.

Julia watched him from the floor where she was sorting sheets of paper into various piles. She sat back on her heels.

"What?" she said. "Don't tell me you sniffed out the perp." She was glad of his company as she worked at restoring order. The thought that the intruders could have made their way up to her apartment and caught her by surprise wasn't something she wanted to dwell on. "I know you'd rather be with Dax tonight but I'm glad you were here. My very own burglar alarm." She rose from her crouched position and scratched him behind the ear.

Callahan yawned hugely and continued to sit on the desk. His eyes blinked slowly once again, and he said, "Yeow."

Julia smiled and returned to sorting receipts, photos, claim forms, and other bits of information. After a couple of minutes, she paused and looked up at Callahan. She watched him patiently waiting then she got up from the floor. "All right, my friend, let's see what's so interesting up here."

She pulled the chair up to the desk and sat, moving

Callahan to the corner of the desktop as she did. It took a few seconds for the computer to boot up. She scrolled through her documents file, hoping to find something that would indicate what the intruders were searching for. After about ten minutes she sat back and drummed her fingertips on the desk. "I give up. Nothing stands out."

She started to return to the mess of files on the floor then decided to check her email. As soon as she opened Gmail, Callahan stood and walked across the keyboard.

"Callahan!" She lifted him down to the floor and shook her finger at him. "Bad kitty!"

Callahan arched his back and walked away on stiff legs, disdain radiating throughout his body.

Julia turned back to the computer screen and discovered the cat, in his prance across the keyboard, had opened an email from Sandra, a long-time friend and the receptionist at her new client's insurance agency. Staring at her from the computer was a handsome man with dark brown eyes and a strong chin.

"Hello. What's this?" She clicked on the image and reduced it from full screen. The photo was on a dating site. *Single, thirty-two, relatively new to the area, antique car enthusiast.*

She studied the image. There was something familiar about that face. Douglas Heinz. Who was Douglas Heinz and where had she seen him before?

* * *

Mitch Lawson stood in the shadow of the Federal style building. The cone of light from the wrought iron lamppost on the corner created night blindness for anyone who might glance in his direction. He had been standing there for well over two hours, his stance relaxed, unmoving. It was a stance learned from years of surveillance duty and one he could maintain for hours if necessary. The alleyway leading down the side of the Georgian house across the street was lit by low lights on the side of the main building, their design not meant for security but rather for their historical aesthetic.

His attention was focused on the carriage house at the end of the alley. It, too, was lit by a gas carriage lamp but the illumination was sufficient for him to determine that no one had come or gone from the building since his arrival.

He glanced down at his watch. It was two o'clock in the morning. He looked up and down the street, alert to any movement. Nothing. He stepped out of the shadows, his head down, the collar of his sports coat turned up, and crossed the street and down the alley, his presence nothing more than another shadow.

There was only one way in or out of the carriage house. Mitch took a pick from his pocket and soon the lock on the Dutch door opened. He slipped into the main living space and stood for a minute, allowing his eyes to adjust to the deeper shades of darkness. There were pinpoints of green light coming from the router of the computer on a desk to the left of the door. Three blue lights from what was probably the television and stereo setup were visible at the end of the room, and from the open door of the bedroom, another faint light source, probably a clock of some kind.

Mitch did a quick reconnoiter of the apartment using a penlight sparingly. The bed had not been disturbed and the bathroom was neat and tidy. He found nothing in the closet out of the ordinary. There were no signs of a meal prepared or eaten in the kitchen. All was spic and span.

At the desk he stood and looked out along the alleyway, his eyes searching every shadow. Finally, he hit the power button and booted up the computer.

The password prompt popped up. What would he use? He began to open desk drawers. In the bottom right drawer, he found a notebook conveniently labeled *passcodes*. Mitch gave a grunt of humor. So much for security.

He went immediately to the browser history. The Bank of Savannah was the only notable site to show up. Nothing unusual there. Under documents he found three files that had been accessed repeatedly over the past thirty days. The activity had been more pronounced in the past week but when he checked into each file, there was nothing that indicated changes to the documents. He sat back in the chair and stared into the darkness, thinking about this. Why monitor these three cases so closely?

From the inner pocket of his sports coat he took out a notepad and pen. He jotted down the names on the files. He started to close out the files and noticed an annotation at the bottom of two of them. They were both assigned to Peter Ryder, a claims adjustor with The Weatherby Insurance Agency, but he, in turn, had requested the involvement of The Hampton Detective Agency.

Mitch closed the documents file and turned off the computer. He sat in the dark letting his vision readjust to the night then stood and left as silently and unnoticed as he had come.

Chapter Two

Julia spent another half hour restoring order to her files then gave up. She yawned, turned out the lights, and went upstairs with every intention of going back to bed but by the time she dug a splinter of glass from her heel and redressed the cuts on her left foot and right arm, it was almost five o'clock in the morning. Her day usually started at six with yoga and copious amounts of coffee. Today she decided to forego the yoga and head straight for the coffee pot.

The phone rang just as she finished her shower. It was six-fifteen.

"Hi, Mom. Right on time."

"Good morning, Julia. Your father is beside himself as I'm sure you're aware. He has Gibbons down in the study grilling the poor man like a defense attorney. You'd better tell me what happened so I can calm the waters."

"I was hoping he wouldn't tell Daddy."

"You know your father worries."

"Yes, Mother, I know. It was nothing really. Someone broke into the office and went through my files."

"Sergeant Gibbons said they trashed the place."

"I prefer to think of it as a very thorough search of my files."

Her mother sighed. "Well, you realize Woodrow will insist on that alarm system now."

Julia groaned. "Mom," the word was a drawn-out plea.

"I'm sorry, Julia. I confess this incident makes me have second thoughts about this new scheme of yours."

"It's not a scheme, Mom. It's a profession."

"Snooping into other people's lives isn't a profession."

Julia chuckled. "No, it's Aunt Ethel."

"Julia!"

"Sorry, Mom."

"Well, you'd best come to breakfast. Better to go ahead and beard the lion and get it over with. Besides, you left your briefcase here last night."

Julia smacked her palm against her forehead. Of all the times to forget her briefcase, this was the worst. She needed it for her meeting with the insurance adjustor later in the morning. All the documents and policy information on a new case with a new client were in it. She would have to face her father at the height of his fright over the break-in.

* * *

The charcoal grey linen sheath struck just the right note. Cool for the September heat, elegant yet professional enough for a business meeting. Julia struggled over the shoes but since she needed to look as grown-up and capable as possible for her encounter with her father, she chose the sherbet orange sling backs and a black envelope handbag. She put her hair up and the gold orb earrings were just enough with the single strand pearl necklace. She checked her appearance in the mirror. "Okay," she said, closed her eyes, and took a deep breath. As she slowly let it out, she opened her eyes. She was ready.

At her parents' home she went in the back way, through the kitchen, and snitched a grape from the fruit bowl. Rosetta gave her a sympathetic look as she headed toward the door to the dining room.

Woodrow Hampton looked over the top of the newspaper and his reading glasses when she entered the room.

Julia hoped the flesh tone of the Band-Aids on her right arm would go unnoticed. She rounded the table and kissed his cheek. "Good morning, Daddy."

"Good morning? Just what, pray tell, is good about it? Amos Gibbons tells me you could have been killed in your sleep."

"Oh, shush, Daddy. You of all people know how dramatic he can be. It was nothing more than a broken pane of glass, someone looking for the office cash, or more likely some kids up to mischief."

"Don't you shush me, young lady. Do you think I just fell off the turnip truck?"

"Now, Daddy, your blood pressure."

"And don't you 'your blood pressure' me. I wouldn't have

to worry about my blood pressure if you hadn't gotten the fool notion into your head that you could meddle in other people's business without any consequences whatsoever."

From the sideboard Julia poured a cup of coffee and put a slice of toast on a plate. "I don't meddle, Daddy. All my job amounts to is research and a lot of paperwork."

"Hah! You think Rocco Sullivan is best pleased that the Mark Rothko he sold to the museum has been declared a fraud on your say so?"

"Not on my say so, Daddy. On the say so of the art curator of the Metropolitan Museum of Art." She sat at the table and began to spread marmalade on her toast.

"Yes, but only because—"

"Woodrow," Audrey Hampton entered the dining room and interrupted the heated conversation between her husband and her daughter, "you're going to be late for the board meeting if you don't get yourself to The Bank."

He rose from his chair. "You needn't think you've heard the last of this." He threw his napkin onto the table and looked from mother to daughter. "Either of you."

Julia stood, and her father took her by the upper arms and gave her a gentle shake.

"You gave us a scare, Little Bit. What would we do if anything happened to you?"

His use of her childhood name was almost her undoing. "Oh, Daddy." She lowered her chin and began to straighten his tie. "Nothing bad is going to happen to me. Savannah is a sleepy little town, not a den of intrigue and high crimes. It was just a random act of mischief. You'll see."

"Well, we're installing that security system." When she started to open her mouth in protest, he held up a warning finger. "I'm not budging on this."

Julia knew when and how to pick her battles, so she smiled sweetly and kissed his cheek. "Of course, Daddy."

Audrey Hampton waited until her husband's footsteps had receded before she launched her own campaign.

"I think we've seen the worst of it. The security system will appease him for now." She poured herself a cup of coffee and took a chair across the table from where Julia had resumed her seat. "But something has come up and I think it's important, for your father's sake, that you attend."

Julia put the last bite of toast back on her plate. She knew this strategy and her mother wasn't a foe so easily vanquished.

"Okay, let me hear it."

Her mother smiled before launching the first foray.

"The Bank is acquiring Low Country Securities. The merger has been finalized and there needs to be a suitable recognition of the occasion."

Julia tried to detect any ulterior motive in this opening salvo. It seemed innocuous enough on the face of it. That was why she knew to be doubly vigilant. Nothing with her mother was ever so benign.

"How suitable?"

"A party at The Club, formal attire, I should think."

"Lots of pomp and circumstance."

Her mother inclined her head slightly. "Exactly. The Bank will absorb the primary executives, give them some title in a nice office."

"And a golden parachute for the dead weight."

"Something like that."

"And why is it important that I be there?"

"Well, this was a hard-won takeover. There's some animosity on the part of one or two of the majority owners so we need to show a united front. Welcome them into the family, so to speak."

"But I have nothing to do with The Bank."

"It's important to your father. Besides, Vincent Richlieu will retain his position as Second Vice-President of Acquisitions."

"Oh, *Mom*. Vinnie Richlieu? Really?"

"Julia, we've known the Richlieus forever. Your cousin Grace is married to Vinnie—Vincent's third cousin on his mother's side." Her mother stirred her now cold cup of coffee. "And you remember Vincent from middle school. He's quite grown out of his acne and braces."

"Mom, I'll get the security system. I'll add flood lights, motion activated lights, to the house. I'll even call every night when I get home. But I draw the line at Vinnie Richlieu."

Audrey Hampton smoothed the immaculate surface of the Irish linen tablecloth. "I understand." She rose from her chair, picked up her cup and saucer, and turned toward the kitchen. "Your father will be so disappointed."

Julia groaned inwardly. Her mother had played her trump card. Her comment was code for a command appearance. She spoke in the language of Southern women. Women who never raised their voices, never quarreled, who never made outright demands. That code was universal throughout the South and it always achieved the desired result.

"And, Julia," her mother said, "wear something with sleeves before it occurs to your father to question all the Band-Aids on your arm."

Chapter Three

Sandra looked up from the reception desk when Julia pushed through the front door of The Weatherby Insurance Agency.

"Julia!" She was all smiles. "Did you get my email?"

Julia, who had just survived a bad night, and it could be argued, a worse morning, was at a loss as to what Sandra was referring.

Sandra must have read the lost expression on her face. She said, "The website. You know. Doug's profile."

"Doug's profile?" Julia frowned then she remembered. "Douglas. Douglas Heinz."

"Yes!" Sandra looked as if she would pop with barely suppressed excitement. "Isn't he a dream?"

Julia smiled at Sandra's enthusiasm and her own

memory of the website photo. "Not bad. If it's a real photo of a real guy. Everyone lies on those sites."

"No, no, no." Sandra shook her head. "He's as real as they come. I know because we posted the profile."

"We?"

"Me and Debbie."

Debbie was the secretary for the claims adjustor for The Weatherby Insurance Agency.

"So who is he?"

"The new guy."

"The new— Wait. What new guy?"

"Well, not new, new. He's been here almost a year."

"Now I see why he looked so familiar. I must have glimpsed him around the office at some point." She dug around in her briefcase and came up with a daily reminder. "I have an appointment—"

"Julia!" Sandra slapped her hands on the desk. "What about Doug?"

Julia raised her gaze from the page of her daily reminder. "What about him?"

"Don't you want to—you know—ping him?"

"Ping him," Julia said in amazement while she silently thought, *matchmakers to the left of me, matchmakers to the right of me*. "I'm not going to date some guy who has to resort to the internet to get someone to go out with him." All the time she was really thinking *loser*.

"But he didn't." Sandra looked crushed.

"I'm sorry," Julia's eyebrows rose in question, "didn't what?"

"He didn't post the profile. We did. Me and Debbie."

"You mean he doesn't know?"

Sandra shook her head.

"Oops."

Julia could see doubt spreading across Sandra's face and wished she had held her tongue.

"You don't think he'll be mad?"

What to say? Julia knew she would be spitting mad if any of her friends pulled such a stunt on her.

"Maybe not. If he's such a great guy I'm sure he'll take the news in the spirit it was intended."

Just then the door to the inner offices of the insurance agency flew open and none other than Douglas Heinz marched into the reception area. "Sandra."

Sandra stood so quickly her chair flew back against the partition wall.

"What are all these messages in my inbox? And what the heck is Couples Connection?"

Julia couldn't help but notice that Douglas Heinz looked even more attractive when his dark eyes flashed with what appeared to be more than a little anger.

"D-d-doug," Sandra stammered. "Douglas Heinz, this is Julia Hampton."

Doug nodded in Julia's direction, then took a breath in preparation for what Julia was sure would be a diatribe at Sandra. But he stopped as if in mid-thought and turned back to Julia.

"Julia Hampton?"

"Yes."

All the anger disappeared from his expression. "The private detective of The Hampton Detective Agency?"

Julia smiled. "One and the same."

"What brings you to The Weatherby Agency?"

"An appointment with Peter Ryder."

"Too bad. I was hoping it had something to do with

the prank Debbie and Sandra have gotten me into."

"Prank?" Julia knew he was flirting, and she liked that he was. Who wouldn't trade Vinnie Richlieu for this *single, thirty-two, fairly new to the area, antique car enthusiast.*

Douglas Heinz revealed a perfect row of pearly whites and said, "It seems I've been languishing on the shelf for too long, in their opinion."

"Ah," Julia said. "So, Couples Connection isn't a marriage counseling service?"

"If it is, the ladies have made a grave mistake."

"How so?"

"I have no wife, no significant other, no better half."

"A pity."

"Not from where I'm standing."

Julia was accustomed to male attention. Doug's flirting didn't make her blush. She realized she was enjoying it. But she was here on business. She smiled at Douglas Heinz then returned her attention to Sandra who was beaming like the mother of a newborn baby.

"Sandra, would you let Peter know I'm here?"

"Oh," Sandra said. "He isn't here. In fact, I can't find him."

"Since when?"

"Yesterday afternoon. He checked in after his morning appointment then was a no-show for his two o'clock."

Doug said, "I saw him just before lunch yesterday. Have you tried his home?"

"Home and cell. I can't reach him anywhere." Sandra frowned. "It's not like him to simply duck out on his appointments."

Julia returned her calendar to her briefcase. "I'll try to reach him and reschedule. Let me know when he checks in."

Doug touched Julia's arm lightly. "How about a cup of coffee? I mean now that your calendar is open."

Julia thought about the disarray still awaiting her at her office but then she looked at the invitation in Doug's eyes and allowed herself to be swayed.

* * *

The night had turned cool for September in Savannah. The following day held a crispness that Julia loved. Autumn was her favorite time of the year. The alfresco tables at Adolpho's had been the perfect choice for the dinner invitation which Julia had—over coffee with Douglas Heinz the previous day —deftly turned into the more innocuous lunch they had just enjoyed. She smiled at her reflection in the mirror of the powder room where she had just reapplied her lipstick. There was potential here, she decided. Doug was witty, intelligent, and a far cry from Vinnie Richlieu.

He waited on the sidewalk outside the entrance to the restaurant and turned to her with a smile as she came through the door. The slant of the autumnal sun etched his face in sharp contrasts of light and shadow. Sunglasses hid his eyes. For an instant his expression brought a wolfish image to Julia's mind. It passed before the thought could fully take hold as he reached out his hand to her and threaded her arm through his.

They turned down the sidewalk in the direction where Doug had parked his classic 1966 Ferrari Spyder a block and a half away.

"So," Doug said as he snugged her arm more securely in the crook of his elbow, "did I pass muster? Table manners up to par? Proper wine selection? Passable meaningless conversation?"

Julia laughed. "You'll do in a pinch."

"Ah." He smiled. "A compliment of the highest magnitude, coming from the daughter of Woodrow Hampton, as in The Bank of Savannah Hamptons?"

Although he posited his statement as a question, Julia felt a slight letdown for she knew that knowledge changed things. She didn't allow her disappointment to show but said in a like teasing manner, "Oh, my, yes. Or as we in the family refer to it, The Bank."

"As everyone in Savannah refers to it as well, probably even in the hallowed halls of Wharton Business School." He sighed. "Worse luck."

Julia kept her tone light and teasing. "Why's that?"

Doug stopped in the middle of the sidewalk and turned to face her as her arm slipped from his. "Because I like you."

"Okay. And why is that bad luck?"

"Pretty girl, old family, rich and powerful daddy. He's probably running a background check on me as we speak."

The smile faded from her expression. "And what will he find?"

Doug lifted his shoulders in a dismissive shrug. "Middle class, state college educated, nose to the grindstone average Joe."

She thought of the expensive classic car he drove. Vulgar as her mother thought the habit, her job had taught her to assign value to rare objects of beauty. The Ferrari was probably worth more than half a million dollars. Doug wasn't such an average Joe as he pretended.

"Well, in that case," she said, the humor returning to

her voice, "you're perfectly safe from Daddy's objections. He knows I'm only interested in equally old family, rich, and powerful contenders."

Doug grinned, and they turned back along their path. "Thank God. I didn't think I could dodge that bullet."

"Well, since you now know you're safe from my feminine wiles, I have a favor to ask."

"A damsel in distress? Is that your ploy?"

"I find it works on occasion."

"Okay," he said, "lead me down the primrose path."

"There's an event I have to attend on Friday evening. One of those fusty old gatherings to grace the anointed with my presence."

"Command performance?"

Julia sighed. "Yes."

"Then I'm at your service. Where and what time shall I pick you up?"

"Black tie at The Club and seven o'clock."

"Black tie, huh. And The Club would be, of course, The Savannah Golf Club."

She smiled. "Of course."

He laughed. "Well, count me—"

The words died on his lips as they came abreast of his car. The pristine red paint had the letters D I C scratched deeply into the hood. A long, keyed scratch traveled down the passenger side from front to back.

"Son-of—" He paled, snatched his sunglasses off, and ran his hand over his eyes as if to erase the image. "What the hell!"

"My God, Doug." Julia stared at the damage. "Who would do such a thing?"

Doug turned from the car, his back to Julia. She saw his

shoulders draw in as if in pain for just a second then his posture straightened, his shoulders squared, and he turned back toward the car. There was a change in his voice when he spoke, a deadly quality that caused Julia to take a small step back. His words belied his expression. "Vandals." He cleared his throat. "Damn fool kids, probably."

"Surely not." Julia's gaze settled on the capital letters across the hood of the car. They were deep and the lines sharp and smooth as if done quickly, as if the perpetrator were in a rage, no hesitation, just violence. Kids would perhaps key the side of the car, maybe even try to steal the Ferrari emblem, but would they be so wrathful as to gouge letters deeply into the hood?

Julia dug into her purse and brought out her cell phone and began dialing. "I'm calling the police."

Doug's reaction was immediate. "No!" He raised his hand, palm toward her in a placating gesture. "No. Let's not get bogged down in legalities. We'll never know who did it and," he sighed and dropped his hand, "it's insured."

She had already punched in 911. "But it has to be documented. You know better than anyone how difficult a claim on a car this rare will be to negotiate." As he started to protest again, she turned slightly from him. The dispatcher was on the line. "Yes, there's been an act of vandalism…" From the corner of her eye, she saw Doug jam his sunglasses onto his face and turn his head from her. She gave the dispatcher the particulars of their location and placed a hand on his shoulder. "I'm sorry, Doug. It's such a beautiful car."

He turned back to face her, shrugged then adjusted the knot in his tie. Before he could speak, an unmarked dark sedan came to a screeching halt in the street on the driver's side of Doug's car.

The tall drink of water who unfolded himself from the driver's seat had Julia's full attention. When he walked around the hood to stand in front of her and Doug, she had to suppress a sigh.

"Hello, Doug. What seems to be the problem?" He removed his Ray-Bans and glanced at Julia then back to Doug.

"Mitchell." Doug rolled his shoulders and squared his stance. "What are you doing here?"

"Heard the call from dispatch." He lifted his hand in a nonchalant gesture. "I was in the area and thought I'd check it out."

Julia took in the dark, nondescript sedan with antennas sprouting from the back and cleared her throat.

Doug looked down at the sidewalk, gave a small shake of his head, then made the introductions. "Julia, this is Mitchell Lawson. Lawson, this is Julia."

Julia inclined her head slightly, taking in Mitch's jeans and plaid shirt, the sleeves rolled back revealing tanned forearms and a serious watch. She let her gaze travel down to long fingers, no ring. "And you know Doug how?"

"College. Looked him up when I got assigned here from Tampa. Heard he was in insurance."

"Assigned?"

Doug smoothed his tie into place. "Mitch is a U.S. Deputy Marshal."

"Oh."

Mitch smiled. "It sounds more dangerous than it is. The truth of the matter is I'm just another paper pusher."

He didn't look like any paper pusher Julia had ever seen. In fact, there was an air of strength and perhaps even a hint of danger about him. "And you needed insurance?"

At that comment, his smile reached his eyes. "Doesn't everybody?" Then he looked down at the Ferrari's hood and said, "Ouch."

Julia let her gaze slide over the damage to the car and frowned. "It just seems so violent, more than some kid keying a car or cutting a ragtop." When she glanced up, she caught Mitch Lawson studying her and she returned his regard with an equally unflinching once over.

He grinned just as a patrol car drew up behind his sedan. Julia felt her face grow hot.

Mitch took out his phone and snapped several photos of the damaged car, slipped it back into his pocket and with a mock salute to Doug, got behind the wheel of the sedan and drove away.

Chapter Four

Mitch sat at his desk, reared back in his chair, and scrolled through the photos he had taken at the scene of the vandalism to Douglas Heinz's Ferrari. The one that held his attention had nothing to do with the car or Doug. When he first stepped around the hood and got a good look at the blonde standing there, the old movie *Rear Window* popped into his head. She was his Grace Kelly. He grunted and sat up straight at his desk. Well, she wasn't *his* Grace Kelly. But who was she, this Julia no-last-name? And what was someone that classy doing with his old friend Doug?

He had to agree with Julia. The damage to Doug's car was not some idle act of destruction for its own sake. It had been personal. Mitch looked across the room at a deputy sitting at another desk. "Hey, Jones. We need to tighten surveillance on Pretty Boy."

Jones looked up from a stack of files on his desk, a scowl on his face. "What's up?"

"Not sure. But someone is very unhappy with him right now. Let's hope it isn't someone from the old neighborhood."

Jones glanced at the stack of files and sighed. "I'm not sure which I hate more, paperwork or surveillance." He stood and caught his jacket off the back of his chair. "Home or office?"

"You take home. I'll send Handel to cover the office."

"And what about you?"

"Legwork."

"Yeah, right."

Mitch grinned and logged into his computer. He did a search for Peter Ryder. A quick background check revealed a fifty-six-year-old native of Savannah employed for the past twenty-three years by The Weatherby Insurance Agency as their in-house claims adjustor. The tax records valued his house at just over two hundred thousand. He drove a four-year-old Ford Explorer. Still making payments on it. No red flags there.

Next, he searched for and found The Hampton Detective Agency. "Well, well, well." So, Julia no-last-name was, in fact, Julia Hampton. The same Julia Hampton who had just been hired by the insurance agency Doug Heinz worked for to investigate two major art thefts. The same Julia Hampton that Dougie had been so reluctant for him to meet.

* * *

The days were getting shorter and the slant of the sun lower in the southern sky. The Italianate building that housed The Weatherby Insurance Agency cast a long shadow across Jefferson Street. Mitch closed the door of the sedan and looked up and down the block. This particular area of the historic district didn't get as much tourist foot traffic as the well-marketed squares. He spotted Handel three buildings down at a sidewalk coffee bar reading a book.

When he entered the building that housed the Weatherby Insurance Agency, he recognized the receptionist from the service's surveillance photos of Doug Heinz. The nameplate on her desk said Sandra Holding. She smiled up at him. "Hello. Can I help you?"

"I'm looking for Peter Ryder. Is he available?"

The corners of the receptionist's mouth turned down and her brow furrowed into a look of concern. "He's not in at the moment. Can someone else help you?"

"Know where I can find him?"

She shook her head. "No." She hesitated then leaned slightly forward. "I'm worried about him. No one has seen him since Tuesday."

"He hasn't been to work?"

"No, and he's not at home either. Debbie went by his house at lunch because he's missed two appointments."

"What about his phone? Cell?"

She shook her head. "Nothing. I've called and called. All I get is his voicemail."

Mitch stared at the detailed woodwork of the arch leading from the foyer into the main offices of the company, his mind elsewhere as he sorted known facts. He looked back at Sandra. "What was he working on when you last saw him?"

She sat back in her chair, a belated look of caution overtaking her concern for her colleague. "And who are you?"

Mitch opened his jacket to reveal the six-star badge clipped to his belt. "U.S. Marshals Service. Mitchell Lawson."

"And why do you want Peter?"

"We have an interest in one of his cases."

She hesitated, then stood. "You need to talk to Mr. Weatherby. But he's out of the office."

"How about Douglas Heinz?"

"Doug? Why do you want Doug?"

Mitch hesitated. "An old acquaintance. Heard his car was vandalized earlier today."

She dropped back into her chair. "Vandalized." She looked up at Mitch. "What's happening around here? Peter missing, Doug's car vandalized." She glanced around as if there were villains lingering in the corners of the foyer. "This is Savannah. Things like this don't happen in Savannah."

Mitch didn't disabuse her of the notion of safety. He couldn't tell her there was a viper in the heart of her quiet, sleepy, little world. He couldn't tell her that viper had been placed there by his own agency.

"I wouldn't worry too much." It was the most he could offer her by way of reassurance. He took a card from his pocket and laid it on the desk. "Have Ryder contact me when he shows up."

* * *

Ryder, for an insurance investigator, wasn't very keen on protecting his own worldly goods. Mitch jimmied the lock on the back door of his home in record time. The house had a stale odor to it, not that of ancient dust and neglect, but rather a sense of absence.

There wasn't much to see in the three-bedroom, bath-and-a-half, house. Though neat and clean, it bore witness to a man living alone. The refrigerator contained a variety of takeout packages, a six pack of beer with one missing, and a bowl of what might have been peaches growing an outstanding crown of mold. A much-used recliner faced a television screen of mammoth proportions. The home office occupied one of the bedrooms. Nothing seemed to be amiss. An antiquated HP computer tower and screen sat on the desk. He opened drawer after drawer of the file cabinets. The manila folders marched along neatly. Mitch looked for files on the three claims he had seen on Doug's computer. There were none. A notepad beside the old-fashioned black telephone was blank, clean of any messages or doodles.

He stood in the middle of the living room and let the house speak to him. It spoke of a lonely man, an ordinary man of limited interests and few, if any, friends.

* * *

It wasn't yet five o'clock when he pulled up to the house on Calhoun Square, but the light was already fading toward twilight. The front door of the building stood open, and a canvas drop cloth trailed across the foyer. A man in well-worn Army fatigues and heavy boots was on his knees beside the French doors leading into a room off the foyer, a putty knife in his hands. He looked up at the sound of footsteps.

Mitch nodded and stepped into the office doorway. Julia sat at a heavy mahogany desk with carved legs and ball-and-claw feet. She was turned sideways to the desk and the door. Her focus centered on a folder in her lap. The lighting in the room was warm and subdued, coming from a small chandelier suspended off-center from the ceiling over a table in the corner and an art deco lamp on the desk. It created a glow around Julia. The sight of her sent a small shock of pleasure through him. The light and her pose brought to mind a painting he had once seen in a museum.

A large gray cat with drooping ears looked up from where he lounged across the cushion of a small sofa covered in a patterned fabric depicting birds. He stood, placed his front legs before him, his rear end rising into the air, spread his toes, and indulged in a major stretch. Then he hopped down from the sofa and approached Mitch, his walk stiff-legged, slow. His scarred right ear twitched as he sniffed the hem of Mitch's jeans.

The movement of the cat drew Julia back from her concentration on the file and she looked up to find him standing there. She closed the file and turned to face the desk. "Hello."

"Ms. Hampton."

"Deputy Lawson." A hint of a smile played across her features. "To what do I owe the pleasure?"

"Peter Ryder." He watched for her reaction.

She frowned. "Yes. I've been trying to catch up with him. We had an appointment yesterday morning, but he wasn't in his office. I've left him a couple of messages but so far, no response." She, in turn, watched Mitch. "Why?"

"A case I'm working. A painting lost in transit." He took the notebook from his inner jacket pocket though he didn't really need to refer to it. "Portrait by a Nicolai Fechin. Shipped from The Palm Beach Auction House two weeks ago. Only an empty crate arrived." He flipped the notebook closed and returned it to his pocket. "Sound familiar?"

"Should it?"

"Only if you're good at your job."

She sighed. "Okay. Yes, I know about it. Peter thought the file needed a second pair of eyes, so he convinced Weatherby to contract me to look into it." She moved the computer's mouse across the pad and the screen came to life with an image of an old man reading a newspaper. "It's one of the many portraits Fechin did of his father."

Mitch walked around the desk to stand at her shoulder. "Nice."

"I prefer some of his other portraits. He did eyes beautifully, so varied and realistic. They give life to his work. In this one you don't really see the eyes."

"You seem to know a lot about this painter."

"About Russian art, Mr. Lawson. My major in college."

"And yet you're a private detective."

"You could say I fell into the job."

"Uh huh." He studied the painting. "What would be the value of something like this?"

"It's hard to say. The buyers of this particular piece, Joshua and Alice Peltier, paid one point two million." She retrieved a form from the folder and handed it to him. "But Fechin's work has gone for much higher prices. In 2011, the MacDougall House in London sold one of his portraits for ten point nine million."

Mitch whistled softly through his teeth.

"That's not the norm for his work. The new Russian billionaires have a taste for Russian artists and apparently two of them got in a bidding war over that particular piece. Though Fechin did the majority of his work in the U.S. after he came here in 1930, places like MacDougall's are profiting from a new awareness of his talent and ethnicity. In the past he was always promoted as an American artist."

"Why MacDougall?"

"They specialize in Russian art. The piece I was telling you about, the one the Russians got in a bidding war over, had sold for just over six hundred thirty thousand a mere seven months earlier."

"Someone made a killing."

"Yes, well art has become the new gold. People are buying for the long- term value. Mainly it's lesser-known artists that buyers hope will appreciate with time. They hope to find the next Van Gogh, an artist who, sadly, never sold a painting during his lifetime."

"Hmm." Mitch handed the report back to her and began a perusal of the room. Over the table in the corner was a painting of a nude woman holding a towel to her chest as she lifted the hair from her neck with her other hand, her head angled enticingly toward the viewer. It was a fetching scene. It was illuminated by a recessed light in the ceiling. He examined it closely. "Is this your own investment in the artists of the future?"

Julia smiled and came to stand beside him. "No. That's actually a Fechin. My great-grandmother gave it to me as a graduation present when I finished undergraduate school."

Mitch filtered that fact through his mental folder on

Julia Hampton. The art, the house on Calhoun Square, the underotated value of everything in the room. What was she doing with the likes of Doug Heinz, better known as Viktor 'Avoska' Letov, the Russian bag man.

"Your great-grandmother has good taste."

"Yes, she did." Julia folded her arms across her waist, tilted her head slightly and studied the painting. "But in this case, she was also lucky. She was a friend of Fechin's. She sometimes modeled for him."

Mitch studied the figure more closely. "Did she now?"

Julia laughed. "I think she was influenced by her name, Mame."

"Maybe the song was influenced by your great-grandmother."

Julia turned her full attention to him. "A fan of Rita Hayworth's?"

He saw a spark of interest in her eyes. "Who isn't?"

"Most people under the age of seventy." She looked back at the painting and sighed. "You would have loved my Gran. She lived in California during the glory days of Hollywood. She could curl your hair with some of her stories."

The sound of a man clearing his throat brought Julia back to the moment. She turned toward the sound. "Oh, Dax. I almost forgot you were here. All done?"

"I'll have to come back in a couple of days to paint it. Need for the glazing to dry." He was in the process of gathering up his tarp. "You need anything else while I'm here?" He cut his eyes in Mitch's direction then looked back at her.

"No, no. It's late. You can finish the repair at the beginning of next week. No need for you to come on the weekend." She opened the top drawer of her desk. "Shall I pay you now for what you've done?"

He shook his head. "We'll settle up when everything's finished to your liking."

"Thanks, Dax. All this threw my plans out the window. I'll see about that vet appointment tomorrow."

He nodded. "You want me to take him with me tonight?"

"If you don't mind," she said, "I'm happy for him to stay with me for now."

Dax's gaze fell on the cat and lingered for a moment. He glanced at the newly repaired door then gave a small nod. "I don't think he'll mind."

"I like his company."

"He's good at that. A good listener."

Julia smiled. "I agree."

Dax nodded again. "Until Monday, then." He took his bundle and left the office.

Mitch walked over to the door and studied the repair. "What happened here?"

Julia waved her hand dismissively. "A break-in two nights ago. Just kids looking for office change or out for mischief."

"Yeah?" Mitch watched as the cat wound between his legs then batted at the door, barely missing the still damp glazing compound. "What did they take?"

"To be truthful, nothing. It has taken me two days to restore order but so far, I haven't found anything missing."

"Trashed the place, did they?" Mitch turned from the door and stared at the painting.

Julia looked up from her desktop. "Yes."

"And left all this expensive art and electronics."

Julia hesitated. "Well, I kind of scared them off."

He turned to her. "You were here?"

She shrugged. "Well, not in the office. I was upstairs. In my apartment. Callahan heard them and woke me."

"Callahan?"

"Yeow." The cat hopped back onto the sofa and began to clean his face.

"Yes. Callahan. As in Dirty Harry?" Julia smiled. "Dax is doing some work for my mother, and I've been tasked with taking the cat to the vet."

"What's wrong with his ears?"

Julia laughed. "Nothing. He's a Scottish Fold." She scratched Callahan under his chin.

"What?"

"It's a breed. They're known for their ears."

Mitch watched the woman and cat. "Uh huh."

Julia laughed. "He's good company. Dax was worried about a bit of a cough he picked up somewhere on the road. We were scheduled for the vet yesterday but the break-in upset my plans."

"The odd jobs guy?"

"Former Army. Travels around from place to place seeing the states."

"How do you know all this?"

"My daddy had him vetted."

"And he has a cat for a traveling companion?"

"Yes."

"There's a first for everything, I suppose."

His attention returned to the repaired office door. The art theft, the missing insurance adjustor, the vandalism to the Ferrari, the break-in, and the pretty lady. Mitch didn't like any of it. And right smack in the middle of all of it was

Avoska, alias Douglas Heinz.

"So, how long have you known Doug?"

Julia returned to her desk, sat, and leaned back in her chair. For a moment she didn't answer. "Your friend from college?"

Mitch nodded.

She straightened the items on her desk, the stapler, aligned with the tape dispenser, the pencils in the holder all slanting in the same direction. "You don't sound like you're from Tampa."

"I'm not."

"Oh?"

"Military brat. I'm from pretty much all over the states, including Hawaii."

"I see."

She still hadn't answered his question. He knew better than to press, to place too much emphasis on the connection. He could feel her clamming up. He would learn nothing more today. He took a business card from his pocket and placed it on the desk then turned toward the open doorway. "If you hear from Ryder, give me a call." He wanted to say more, to warn her of the danger, but he couldn't afford to show his hand. So, he simply walked out of the building and into the descending night.

Chapter Five

Julia picked up the card and read it. Then she moved to the window and watched as Mitch Lawson stood on the sidewalk outside her house, unmoving, staring into the darkness.

She hated to think she was so fickle, but from the moment he had stepped into her office she had forgotten all about Doug Heinz. That is, until Lawson brought him up. What was it between those two? She had sensed the tension in Doug on the street earlier in the day when Mitch arrived in response to her 911 call. At the time she brushed it aside as anger over the vandalism. Now she wasn't so sure. It now seemed more than a little suspicious that Mitch would have shown up at the scene, and so quickly at that. She remembered he had taken photos of the damage.

Why would he do that? At best, it was a matter for the local police. And now, he was asking questions about her relationship with Doug.

He had come to her in search of information on the theft, or so he said. Why did she feel there was more to it than that? She sighed. Her father's concern over her safety was beginning to take its toll. All these unanswered questions didn't help matters. She had brushed off the break-in to everyone but now she could admit to herself a little niggle of fear. After the break-in, Peter Ryder had disappeared and a U.S. Deputy Marshal had arrived on the scene, tight lipped and watchful. What was really going on?

She placed the card on her desk and started to tidy up the files on the table in the corner of her office. Callahan dropped to the floor from the sofa and padded across to her desk. He jumped to the chair then the desktop.

"What have I told you about my desk, Callahan?" Julia stopped what she was doing, a stack of files in her hand.

Callahan batted at the card with his paw, moving it around on the desktop. Then he sat on his haunches and blinked slowly three times. "Yeow."

Julia replaced the files on the table and crossed the room to stand looking down at Callahan. She picked up the card. "Okay. So, what's the message? Friend or foe?"

Callahan began to purr, his eyelids drooping to half-mast.

Julia started scratching him under his chin. His eyes closed, and the purring grew to the sound of a small cement mixer. "I think you like him."

Callahan's eyes opened to golden slits, then closed again. A final judgment, Julia thought, on the merits of one Mitchell Lawson, U.S. Deputy Marshal.

* * *

Julia tapped Mitch's card against her chin. The key, she thought, was Peter Ryder. As soon as the claim was assigned to her, he disappeared. True, it had been only a little over forty-eight hours since anyone had last seen him, but the timing was suspicious.

She picked up the desk phone and dialed his home. The burring ring of the phone went on for a long time and she sighed. Peter was old fashioned in that he refused to have an answering machine. The only people who needed to reach him, he had once told her, were calling him on business and they could darn well contact him at the office or on the company issued cell phone. It was a sad comment on Peter's life, but there it was.

The problem was he wasn't answering either of those devices. How did you go about tracking someone down who had no life outside the job?

What was it Sandra had said? He had missed his last appointment on Tuesday. Julia reached for the phone again but this time she called the receptionist.

Peter's last appointment, according to Sandra, concerned a claim about stolen assets from an estate just prior to the auction date. There hadn't been any art involved but a Bentley was on the auction block as well as quite a bit of jewelry. It was the jewelry that was missing and it was covered by a policy written by The Weatherby Insurance Agency. The deceased was from Savannah and his home in the historic district would be part of the auction.

Julia picked up the file she had found with the two art cases. When she first discovered it earlier in the day, she had assumed Ryder had given it to her by mistake. She knew the family and was aware of the upcoming auction, but the stolen jewelry wasn't part of her contract with the insurance agency. It had to be a mistake. Her field of expertise was art, more particularly, Russian art. She read the form and scanned the list of stolen items and put the file aside.

The second case assigned to her could possibly have a tie-in to the Fechin theft, she thought. Apparel once worn in 1868 by King Christian IX of Denmark to the christening of Nicholas II, future Czar of Russia, had gone missing in transit from a private owner in New York. It disappeared enroute to the Telfair Museum as part of a display on Russian art.

Julia had given the file a quick read when it landed in her in-box. Because it was the lesser of the two claims she had contracted to review with the insurance agency, she had looked more in-depth at the Fechin theft. She had spoken with the owners on Monday, but they were unable to meet with her. Joshua and Alice Peltier were on their way to Cozumel for a granddaughter's wedding. The Fechin was to have been a wedding gift for the newlyweds.

She took the two files and her laptop to the table in the corner of the office and began a systematic review of the cases.

Forty-five minutes later she knew two disturbing facts. The first thing that caught her attention was the method of delivery. Usually, such rare and valuable items were handled by a select few and well-insured companies, who were experts in the field of crating, temperature control, and proper handling of delicate items. Even more telling, a piece as valuable as the Fechin portrait would be escorted by a representative of the company from the moment it left the gallery to its final delivery point. In this case, the Peltiers had requested it be delivered to the Telfair Museum so it could be evaluated before they sent it on to their granddaughter.

The second thing was the mode of transport. Both pieces had come by way of a tanker ship. Normally they would be delivered by a temperature-controlled van or truck, depending on their size, or they would be sent by air freight.

Climate control was a crucial aspect of transporting and storing both the clothing items and the painting. Perhaps the individual owner of the apparel might not have been aware of the significance of these precautions but the auction house in Palm Beach should certainly have known better as should the transport company out of Miami. It was possible that a temperature-controlled shipping container was used but there was no indication of that fact in the documents on file.

She would need to speak with each party responsible for such an important task. The clock in the foyer chimed six o'clock. It was too late an hour to contact the representative of the shipping company, one Renee Slavoska. Julia made a notation of the office number on the inside cover of the file jacket and placed it on her desk for attention first thing in the morning. She took a light sweater from an armoire in the corner of the office and turned out the lights. A nice walk down to the river was what she needed.

* * *

Something isn't quite right with the shadow two doors down and across the street. The security lights on the first house deepen the shadows of its neighbor but something is there, I sense it.

"Well, come on." *Julia is standing at the open door of the office. She has put on a light sweater.*

She claps her hands at me as I watch her from the window. My ears flatten. She did not just clap her hands at me as if I were a mere dog!

"Callahan!" *She starts across the room toward me.* "Upstairs with you."

I drop from my vantage point on the back of the small sofa, slip between her legs before she can catch me, and head out the door and up the stairs. It's about time she called it a day. I'm starving.

In the apartment she turns on lights, hits the play button on the answering machine, and opens the refrigerator.

A man's voice almost purrs from the machine. I flick my ear.

"Sorry about this afternoon, Julia. The damage to my car threw me for a loop. I'm really a nice guy when you get to know me." *A deep chuckle follows this self-aggrandizement. I flick my ear again. Julia smiles and I flatten my ears.*

"So," *The Voice continues,* "I'll see you tomorrow night." *Julia smiles broader.*

"Yeow!" Enough is enough. Besides, my afternoon snack is now only a faint memory and the dinner hour is fast approaching.

Julia seems to regain her senses and she turns her smile in my direction. "Hungry?"

Seriously?

She takes a container from the refrigerator. My ears whip forward at the rasp of a lid being pried from a metal container. My thoughts rush instantly to sardines in mustard sauce, potted meat, or, in a pinch, plain old tuna fish.

It's none of those things. In fact, it isn't even the plain but highly edible Vienna sausage. The dish she places before me has a harsh odor, a gummy texture, and what looks like a green pea trapped in its gelatin-like substance.

There is hunger and there is starvation. Neither would move me to eat this unidentifiable mush. I lift my tail in rigid declaration of my feelings on the matter and stalk from the room to assume my post at the bedroom window.

Julia appears in the doorway. "What?" *She has the can from which the offensive mush has been provided.* "It says gourmet right here on the label."

I ignore her, not because of the ridiculous defense of her dinner offering, but because the shadow a few doors west and across the street is on the move. I shift my body weight onto my forepaws and press my nose to the glass of the window as the shadow walks toward Abercorn. He's almost directly across the street.

Julia turns from the room and her words are lost to me as I decide on a course of action. I need to know the intent of this silent watcher. I limbo under the edge of the open window and trot along the molding to the canopy over the door of the building. I drop onto the awning, from there to the top of the brick fence adjacent to the house, and then the ground.

My quarry has turned up Abercorn but there's no fear that I'll lose him. I am as a cat in the wild in pursuit of the mysterious figure who keeps watch over Julia's home and office. I'll discover his identity and unravel the reason behind all these nocturnal shenanigans at Number 159, West Taylor Street, or my name isn't Callahan.

I'm upon him in a flash of powerful hind legs and feline stealth. He has stopped, staring down the street at nothing I can see. I catch his scent and the fur on my neck lies down and I relax. It's only The Lawman and it's as if he is trying to make a decision. He shakes his head and continues up Abercorn Street then stops again at the sight of me.

"This place is crawling with cats."

I lift my tail to full mast and stalk ahead of The Lawman.

Surely, he isn't so dull he can't recognize me. True, we've only just met but he must see the distinguished carriage of my person, the thickness of my fur, and the unmistakable gold of my eyes.

"Escaped, have you?"

I hardly consider my decision to investigate the surveillance of my temporary residence an "escape," but I do admit Julia won't be pleased about my activity. She's taken it upon herself to poke her nose into my health, which is just fine, thank you very much.

Cough? What cough? It's simply that I find the repeated meals of Spam unappetizing. I mean, when you're on the road like me and Dax, you make do with what you have. But Spam? What is it anyway? I don't think I've ever seen a spam. If the animal is as uninspiring as it's meat, then I don't think I want to meet one. It's probably a relative of the armadillo. I wonder if that's what armadillo tastes like?

Besides, Lil the Librarian pulled a fast one and took me to the vet not two years before my decision to go adventuring with Dax. I'm fit as a fiddle. Another of those impossible human sayings that are incomprehensible. How is it that a fiddle is fit, I ask you?

The sound of a heavy, well-made door closing draws my attention and that of The Lawman to Julia's house. We look back and watch as she locks and double checks the door. I sense in The Lawman the same indecision I'm suffering; to follow or not to follow.

As she walks down the three steps to the walkway, he moves in her direction a couple of steps then stops. He takes out his cell phone and places a call.

"Do you have eyes on Pretty Boy?"

Interesting. Who is this Pretty Boy, I wonder?

"Yeah," *he continues, then a brief pause followed by a grunt.* "Okay. Stick like a tick."

My ears flick forward. A more unpleasant prospect I can't imagine. Pretty Boy is definitely in disfavor with our Lawman.

The Lawman watches as Julia crosses the street and walks in the direction of the river. She's on the same course as we are but on the opposite side of Abercorn. The Lawman glances left and right then steps into a recessed entry to a garden. His actions pique my curiosity. Why doesn't he want to be seen by Julia? He waits until she's a block ahead then follows on his original course. I look up and see the flashing neon of an eating establishment. I give Julia one last look. My stomach rumbles. I'm torn but then I reason that Julia is smart, competent, and in no immediate danger.

I hurry after The Lawman who has clearly forgotten Julia in favor of food. I sprint to his side before the door of the restaurant can close on my tail. I must, after all, keep up my strength if I'm to be on my game. This breaking and entering business of her office and the arrival of the long arm of the law on the scene means something is up. Whatever it is, The Lawman isn't too concerned.

Chapter Six

Julia liked to walk the streets of the city after dark. The softly lit buildings and street corners gave old Savannah an added charm. To her it spoke of a time of elegance, manners, and beauty. She had been in love with the architecture of her hometown all her life. She felt safe and comforted by its familiarity. It was her habit to wander the area when she was dealing with a knotty problem: an interior design dilemma, a hovering father, and a missing colleague.

She crossed over Bay Street near the Old Cotton Exchange and was walking across the pedestrian bridge that connected to the buildings above the old cobbled streets leading down to the river when she heard a man's voice raised in anger. He spoke with a heavy accent that made his words unclear and the only phrase she understood was "you'll pay or else." She looked over the railing and saw two men standing in the edge of the street light's glow, just outside the passage that ran under the shops on Factors Walk to River Street.

Something was familiar about the taller of the two men. Just as she was about to walk on, he turned to scan the immediate area and she realized it was Doug Heinz.

Julia quickly stepped back from the railing. She didn't want to appear to be spying on him and yet something about the tone of the exchange between the two men made her linger just out of view.

Doug said something in a low placating tone of voice and the stranger gave a guttural grunt of impatience and stalked away through the tunnel arch and out of sight. As Doug moved toward the steep stone stairs leading up to Bay Street where Julia stood, she made a quick decision. For some reason she didn't want to encounter him just now. She turned up the collar of her sweater and caught the walk signal at the traffic light. Once across the street, she ducked into the lobby of the Holiday Inn. She took the elevator to the rooftop pool and stood looking out across the river.

What was it about Doug's conversation with the stranger that bugged her? It brought to mind that fleeting image of him outside the restaurant earlier in the day. The image of a wolf had lingered in the back of her mind. There had been a hint of something wild, dangerous, in his expression.

Julia shook her head and chuckled at her thoughts. A disagreement between two men didn't mean anything more than that—a simple disagreement. Besides, the hint of untamed recklessness was probably what had attracted her to Doug in the first place. She sighed and recognized that thought was tantamount to admitting she had a type, just as her father claimed.

She inhaled deeply of the crisp fall air and watched a ship being maneuvered up river by tugboats. Her mind drifted back to Peter's disappearance. Deep in her gut she felt it had something to do with her new cases. He had suspected something or he wouldn't have involved her. And it was after his appointment with the Director of Cultural Events for the Telfair Museum about the missing apparel that he had dropped off the radar. She would take up the trail there.

With another sigh she turned from the view of the river to retrace her steps back to the street below. Tomorrow she would arrange a visit with the director but for now she needed to find something that finicky cat would eat. The fur ball had a no interest in cat food. Maybe a little sushi would do the trick.

* * *

Mitch looked down at the Scottish Fold trying to slip through the door of Clary's Cafe. He paused for a split second then decided on a sidewalk table. It was clear the cat planned to be his dinner companion.

The waiter paused when he saw the pair of golden eyes peering at him from just above the level of the linen clad tabletop.

"He's with me," Mitch said as he perused the menu without looking up at the waiter. "We'll have the Roquefort Burger, extra meat patty, extra cheese." He handed the menu to the young man still gaping at Callahan. "Rare on the burger and an extra plate."

As the waiter took the menu with a vague nod, Mitch turned his full attention on the cat.

"Just so you know, I'm a dog man."

Callahan flicked his scarred right ear and turned his profile to Mitch with a posture that said the tolerance was mutual. Mitch chuckled deep in his throat as his phone emitted a soft beep. He read the text and frowned as he rose to his feet.

The waiter appeared at his elbow with a glass of water and silverware wrapped in a napkin.

Mitch took out his wallet and dropped a twenty and a five on the table. He turned to the waiter. "Feed the cat."

Both the waiter and Callahan stared at Mitch.

"And you," he said to the cat, "go home."

The cat and boy stared after Mitch as he hurried toward a dark sedan parked at the corner of the block, texting as he went.

By the time Mitch reached Bay Street there was no sign of Julia or Doug. Jones had texted him the moment Julia arrived on the scene. The idea that she had turned up at a clandestine meeting between Doug and one of his low-life associates pricked at Mitch. What was she doing there and who was the stranger? Jones hadn't recognized him but was running a facial recognition search. They would have an identity soon enough if he was in any law enforcement database.

Mitch strolled along Factors Walk and took the stone steps down to River Street. There was no sign of Doug or Julia in any of the restaurants or shops along the riverfront. He made his way back up to Bay Street and stood on the corner of Bryan and Bay Streets for a brief minute then entered the lobby of the Holiday Inn.

The young woman at the reception desk sat up straighter and smiled broadly as Mitch approached.

"May I help you?"

Mitch was aware of a certain appeal to the opposite sex when he put forth the effort. The corner of his mouth lifted in a sheepish grin as he brought his elbow to rest on the countertop.

"It appears I've lost my..." he hesitated for a split second as he assessed the eagerness with which the young woman regarded him. "My sister."

The receptionist touched her hair lightly and her smile widened. "Are the two of you guests here at the hotel?"

"No. No, we're local."

At this admission the receptionist folded her arms, rested them on the countertop and leaned toward Mitch. "So, you think she might be here because..." Her voice trailed off in an unspoken question.

"We were supposed to meet on this corner nearly twenty minutes ago."

"Okay. Tell me about this sister. What does she look like?"

"Grace Kelly."

"What?"

"She looks like Grace Kelly."

"Who's Grace Kelly?"

Mitch gave a small shake of his head. "Never mind. I'm looking for a blonde, hair done up. Slender, dancer's posture. A little taller than you." He smiled at the receptionist. "Seen anyone like that in the last twenty minutes?"

"Yes. I think so." The woman removed her elbows

from the counter and stood with her best posture. "Took the elevator. I thought she was a guest."

Mitch frowned. "Where would a non-guest go?" He looked around the lobby at the reception area, an opening leading to a bar that was closed. "What's on the upper levels?"

"Rooms." The receptionist's expression brightened. "And the pool. On the rooftop."

"Thanks." Mitch gave the woman a smile and turned to the elevators. He got off on the top floor and was greeted by the hint of a fragrance that was already imprinted on his senses. It was her perfume, the one he had noticed on both encounters with Julia. The scent held a promise of something expensive, classy. Something definitely beyond his reach.

There was no one on the rooftop. The lights illuminated the pool from below as the surface rippled slightly in the mild breeze. Mitch stood at the railing along the roofline watching the pedestrian traffic below on Bay Street, the lights in the shops and restaurants along Factors Walk, the outline of the Talmadge Memorial Bridge to the west, and the inky darkness that defined the river. It was an excellent vantage point from which to view the activity below. Was that why Julia had chosen it? Had she been meeting Doug Heinz or spying on him? What did she know?

* * *

Julia rode the elevator down to the lobby, Callahan's dinner menu on her mind. She was halfway to the door onto Bryan Street when she realized the receptionist was trying to get her attention. She stopped and turned to the woman hurrying toward her.

"I'm so glad I caught you," she said. "Your brother just went up to the top floor looking for you."

"My brother?"

The receptionist smiled and rolled her eyes. "I know. Twenty minutes late, right?" She shook her head. "I'd be ready to kill him, too."

Julia frowned. Had Doug seen her after all? Why would he claim to be her brother? Or was someone following her? Too many odd things had happened since she was hired for these new cases. She felt a little frisson of panic. She took a breath and exhaled slowly as she smiled at the receptionist. "Oh, I'm ready to kill him, all right." She paused just long enough to give the impression she was deciding what punishment her errant brother deserved. "Do me a favor," she said. "Don't let on you saw me leave. It'll serve him right to wonder what happened to me."

Julia slipped through the doors to the parking bay just as the elevator opened and Mitch stepped into the lobby. She was stunned to realize the deputy had been spying on her—stunned and outraged. She watched with pleasure from the protective cover of the parking bay as he extricated himself from the very determined receptionist.

She debated walking away but she was too angry. As he stood outside the hotel staring at the business card the receptionist had forced upon him, she stepped out of the shadows and stopped just behind and to the right of him.

"Find your sister?" Her voice was surprisingly calm and mildly inquisitive even to her own ears.

Mitch swung around to stare at her.

"That, of course, is assuming you have a sister." Her voice was losing some of its calm composure as she watched him slip the business card into his pocket. "Because I know you couldn't be looking for me." She felt the color rising up her throat to her face. "The last time I checked I'm an only child."

Mitch recovered with no hint of embarrassment. "Good to know," he said.

Julia fought to tamp down her anger. "So, you want to tell me why you were spying on me? Did you follow me here?"

"I'm not spying on you and I didn't follow you here." He watched her reaction to his words and when she simply raised an eyebrow, he continued. "In fact, I was just about to feed your cat when I got a, uh, business call."

"Feed my cat!" His comment made her so mad Julia almost stuttered the words. "Of all the—that is such a bald-faced lie I don't even know how to respond."

Mitch continued to watch her for a moment longer then said, "I don't lie, at least not when it matters. And I didn't follow you here. I just happened to discover that you were in the area and wanted to make sure you were all right."

"How did you *happen* to discover that I was in the area? And why wouldn't I be fine? I'm an adult, perfectly capable of taking care of myself. I don't need the U.S. Marshals Service looking over my shoulder."

"No, no, you don't." Mitch held up his hand in a placating gesture. "I guess I just wanted to see you."

"Oh." Julia was so caught off guard by his comment that she was having difficulty changing gears. It took her a second to realize he had glibly skipped over her questions.

"Why don't I walk you home and I'll tell you what I can."

"You were spying on someone else." Her eyes widened. "You were spying on Doug."

"Not me personally." Mitch sighed. "Please, let me walk you home."

Julia knew that Mitch's declaration that he wanted to see her was an attempt to cover up the fact he had been spying on her, if not for her own sake, then because of Doug. All her life she had been watched in the guise of coddling and cossetting. The need to escape the loving but watchful eye of her father had almost caused her to take a job as an art curator in Boston after graduation. Now, especially since her career had taken a direction her father disapproved of, she felt her every movement was under scrutiny.

"Look," Mitch said, "you have questions and I need to see you safely home. Why not kill two birds with one stone?"

Why did he have to be so logical, so calm—so *assuming*. But he had her attention and as with her father, Julia knew when to change tactics.

"Fine." She turned south on Bryan Street as Mitch fell in step beside her. They walked a block in silence. Julia finally couldn't stand it any longer. "Well?"

"Well, what?"

"Honestly!"

Mitch chuckled. "What do you want to know?"

"Who were you following tonight?"

"I wasn't following anyone. I was trying to have dinner."

"I'm not the hotel receptionist, Mr. Lawson."

"Indeed, you are not, Miss Hampton. And call me Mitch."

"Okay." Julia said. "Let me rephrase my question. Who

is the U.S. Marshals Service following?"

When he started to speak, she held up her hand to silence him. "And what does it have to do with me?"

"Well, I can't disclose details of an ongoing investigation…"

Julia stopped in her tracks, hands on hips, and glared at him.

"But," he continued, "I can tell you the disappearance of Peter Ryder is of major concern as is your connection to his last two cases."

"The two late nineteenth century Russian cases."

Mitch took her arm and set them back to walking. "A curious but descriptive choice of reference."

"Not so curious," Julia said. "Both claims are connected to Russian history."

"Why do you think Ryder called you in on these particular cases? Do you think it was because of your expertise in Russian art?"

Julia gave a small shake of her head. "Not really. The provenance of the items isn't in question. I think what troubled him is that the seller of the Fechin and the owner of the clothing used unconventional delivery methods for pieces of this value."

"Was the clothing that valuable?"

"Not so much except from a historical perspective. These items are irreplaceable in that they were the personal belongings of a figure from history worn to the christening of the future czar of Russia." She frowned. "That, to me, is the key. I've been thinking about our conversation earlier about the two Russians in a bidding war for a different Fechin painting. What are the odds that two items of Russian origin should go missing at almost the same time and in the same city?"

"History, then, not art."

"Both claims are connected to history and art, but the fact that the clothing links to roughly the same period in history as the Fechin stands out to me. Is there a link there? I don't know."

"Was Fechin a sympathizer with the Romanovs?"

"His early training was with the Kazan Art School, but his father was merely a craftsman who worked in wood and metal. Fechin later attended the Imperial Academy in St. Petersburg but I doubt there was any deep affection for the Czar and the royal families. Like so many in the aftermath of the revolution, he fled to the United States to escape the turbulence and violence. There was a great famine in 1921. He and his family were rescued by the American Relief Administration. He was one of the fortunate ones. In large part, I suspect, because of his art."

Mitch was quiet for the remainder of the block then he said, "So the question is, what is our thief collecting— history or art?"

Julia's mind had been chasing the answer to that question all evening. If they could pin down the answer to the *what*, she felt sure they could discover the who and the how. She stopped again as she realized she had mentally linked her investigation with Mitch's. And he had said *our* thief.

"What?" Mitch stood watching her.

She diverted her gaze and saw the neon sign for Takee-Outtee Sushi Bar. "Callahan."

"What about him?"

She moved toward the take-out café. "He won't eat cat food and he's eating me out of house and home. I thought

I might tempt him with some sushi."

She turned to see Mitch standing in the middle of the sidewalk watching her. He had told her he had been feeding the cat earlier in the evening, but Callahan was securely at home in her apartment. "Are you hungry?"

"For sushi?"

He began to close the distance between them with that walk—that walk that was just so—him. Julia came back to earth and cleared her throat. "Yes, sushi."

He shook his head. "I like my beef rare and my fish cooked."

She wondered what else he liked then took herself firmly in hand. "Good to know," she said.

His mouth didn't move but she saw the smile in the subtle changes in his face, changes you couldn't point out but there all the same. The cause of the smile, she realized, was her use of the exact same words he had used earlier.

Chapter Seven

When they reached Calhoun Square, they found the gray cat sprawled on his side across the doormat. He flicked his tail but made no effort to move.

"Callahan!" Julia stared down at him, a note of alarm in her voice. "How on earth did you get out?"

Mitch stood on the middle step of the porch and decided the cat had eaten the entire Roquefort burger, both patties by the look of him. He appeared to be in a food coma. He had the good sense not to comment.

Julia held up the bag that contained the sushi and gave it a gentle shake. The sound of the container against the paper of the bag caused the cat to flick his ear once more but nothing else.

"Callahan." Julia shook it again. "I've brought you dinner."

Callahan opened his eyes to slits of gold then closed them again.

"Well," Julia said, "you are impossible to please."

"I think he likes his beef rare, too." Mitch forced his words to sound matter-of-fact and he refused to let himself smile.

Julia's forehead furrowed with lines of indignation. "You could have told me."

"I did. You didn't believe me."

"Well, you should have been more persistent."

"I don't like repeating myself."

Julia made no reply. She stepped over Callahan to insert the key in the lock. The door swung open on silent hinges.

Mitch gently eased her out of the doorway. He took his gun from the shoulder harness beneath his jacket and pushed the door all the way open with his booted foot.

Callahan chose that moment to revive and he sauntered past Mitch to the office door. It was intact, no broken panes, and securely locked. Then the cat headed up the stairs toward the apartment on the second floor. Mitch followed, motioning for Julia to stay in the foyer.

At the top of the stairs the cat sat outside the door. It was closed and as Mitch quietly and carefully turned the doorknob, he discovered that it was also locked. He took the penlight from his inside jacket pocket and examined the area around the lock. Someone had made a very discreet effort to trip it. He stepped back down the stairs to the half landing and motioned for Julia to join him. When he held out his hand for her keys, he realized she was trembling. He closed his fingers over her hand and gave it a reassuring squeeze before he took the keys and returned to the top of the stairs to open the door.

Callahan strolled into the entryway of the apartment and turned left toward the front of the building. He hopped up on the window ledge and stared out the window.

Mitch went room to room, checking for an intruder. When he opened Julia's closet door he simply stood and stared. It was a room, arguably as large as his apartment. Clothing ran along two walls. At one end a dressing table with tri-fold mirrors stood against the wall. Angled shelves with row upon row of shoes flanked the dressing table. On the opposite wall, a Vault Pro safe had obviously been custom built to fit the width of the room. He wondered what she could possibly keep in a safe that big. The center of the room contained an adjustable, free-standing, full-length mirror and a large, rectangular ottoman upholstered in some kind of fur under a crystal chandelier. It was the most amazing closet he had ever seen. He whistled softly between his teeth and closed the door.

There was no sign that anyone had been inside the apartment. He paused as he was leaving the bedroom and looked at the very large bed dominating the room. He inhaled Julia's fragrance, which lingered on the air, then he went back to the apartment door and ushered her inside.

"Are you sure you locked the front door?" He knew that she had but it was a question he had to ask.

"Yes." She turned right into the kitchen and set the take-out bag on the butcher block island. "Since the break-in I've been obsessive about it, double checking and then checking again."

She looked very pale. Mitch moved to the stove and checked the kettle for water. He turned on the burner and busied himself looking for cups, spoons, teabags. "No one got into the apartment. You needn't worry about that."

"How can you know? I don't know how they got in downstairs. Or if they've been in the office again." She pulled a long, curved, tortoise shell, slightly dangerous looking object from her hair and it fell in loose waves to her shoulders.

"I just know." He watched her run her fingers through her hair. "It's a talent, I guess you'd say. Comes from years on the job." He hesitated. "Do you want to call the police?"

"God, no." She sat on a stool at the kitchen island. "My father is ready to dig a moat around the building. If he heard about this, he'd probably have me forcibly moved back home."

"Is there anyone you could stay the night with?"

Julia jumped as the kettle began to scream. Then she took a calming breath. "No." She stood and began making tea. "I don't want a babysitter and I'm not going anywhere. No one is going to scare me out of my home."

Mitch leaned against the kitchen doorframe and hitched his thumb into the waistband of his jeans. "Uh huh."

Julia looked up from the tea preparations. "I mean it, Deputy Lawson. This is all related to the thefts I'm investigating. All I have to do is find out who's behind them. Problem solved."

"That easy, huh?"

Julia sighed and took a fresh lemon from the refrigerator and sliced it. "I don't expect you to believe I'm good at my job. I really don't care what you think. But I haven't failed a client yet and I know what I'm doing."

Mitch pushed away from the doorframe and took the cup of tea she offered. He was a coffee drinker, but he said nothing and sipped the hot brew. "Okay, you know your business and I know mine. I also know where all this is leading. It's obvious that whoever's behind these thefts is Russian or has connections to markets specializing in Russian art." He set his cup on the island. "And there are some nasty mafia types operating all up and down the eastern coast."

"Why would you assume the mafia is involved?"

"I'm not." He paused, trying to decide how much he could tell her.

"But you are." Julia set down her cup. "It has something to do with whatever brought you to my door, and don't tell me it was stolen art."

Mitch pinched the bridge of his nose and sighed. "Okay. I can say that an ongoing investigation may be overlapping with these art heists."

"How?"

"I can't say anything about the particulars, but the disappearance of Ryder is a problem."

"And you think Doug's involved."

"Only in that he wrote both policies."

"Do you think he did this?"

"There's no reason to think so at this moment. I'm just trying to see the big picture, and the fact that Doug's the agent may be an unfortunate coincidence."

"What made your men decide to follow him?"

"The thing with the car. It doesn't sit right."

"I agree." Julia took her cup to the sink and emptied it. "It seemed personal."

Mitch crossed the kitchen and placed his empty cup in the sink. "That's how it struck me. There could be a number of reasons, from a jilted woman to a gambling debt, but it bears looking into."

"So, what do we do?"

Mitch grinned. "We?"

"Our cases are connected. It would be foolish not to collaborate."

Mitch liked the idea of collaborating with Julia Hampton but that wasn't really an option. She was no match for the likes of Doug and his mafia cronies. But perhaps, under the guise of cooperation, he could keep an eye on her, could keep her safe.

"Why don't I take a stroll around the block, see if there's any sign of your visitor." He paused in the kitchen doorway. "Lock up behind me. I won't be long."

Julia crossed her arms at her waist and nodded.

When he got to the front door of the building, Mitch examined it carefully with his penlight. The lock was new, no scratches on the metal, so it hadn't been picked that he could tell. The door had been repainted after the initial break-in. There was still the faintest odor of fresh paint. It was unmarred.

He checked the French doors to the office. They were firmly locked; the putty Dax had used to secure the new panes still tacky. There was no sign of an attempt to break in. Whoever had tried to gain entry into Julia's apartment had a key to the main door of the building but not one to the apartment itself. They hadn't attempted to enter the office. Whatever they were looking for they didn't expect to find there. What were they looking for?

The streets around Julia's house were quiet except for an occasional pedestrian. No one caught his eye as suspicious. He scanned the alleyways, alcoves, and darkened doorways. He found no one lurking in any of the parked vehicles. No cars cruised slowly around the area.

Mitch completed the circuit of outlying streets to a

two-block radius around Julia's house. He stood on the sidewalk on the opposite side of the street and looked up to see the silhouette of the gray cat standing watch at the window.

* * *

Julia checked the lock on the apartment door after Mitch left. She then went around to all the windows and closed and locked them.

Callahan protested with a plaintive *yeow* when she moved him so she could close the bedroom window.

"Complain all you want. I'm on to your tricks. No more shenanigans from you tonight."

Callahan looked up at her then began to thread his way around her legs. She picked him up and held him close to her chest. He rubbed his head against the underside of her chin and began to purr.

"Oh, you're ready to make up, are you?" She scratched under his chin and took him to the sofa. The rumble in his throat began to work its magic.

By the time Mitch rang the doorbell Julia had reasoned away the fear that had gripped her when the front door swung open of its own accord. Maybe she hadn't secured the lock properly when she went out. Her mind had been on the case, trying to decide whether or not two thefts of Russian art within a few weeks of each other could be a coincidence.

At the sound of the doorbell Julia stirred from her reverie. She realized Callahan had abandoned her to resume his vigil at the window.

She sighed and pulled herself out of the comfort of

the sofa and checked the security camera. Mitch stood on her front stoop, his face in profile. She sighed again. He was a handsome man. After a long dry spell in her social life, it was suddenly raining men; handsome, sexy, and possibly dangerous men. A little shiver ran down her spine as she pressed the door release button.

* * *

Julia awoke with a strategy in mind. Her first call was to her father to inquire whom he would recommend for a security system. This simple request served to appease Woodrow Hampton and for him to recognize she was appeasing him. If he thought for one second she felt she needed the security, he would station armed men on all four corners of her house.

The call also allowed her to question him about Alphonse Chapman, the Director of Special Events for the Telfair Museums. He was the mastermind behind the scheduled Russian art exhibit.

'Chappie,' according to her father, was a trust fund baby who spent an inordinate amount of time tracing his ancestry then boring all his acquaintances with his findings.

Julia had met Chappie at various functions involving the arts and the Historical Preservation Society. What she needed from her father was the backstory, or as Aunt Ethel would say, the down and dirty.

Other than the fact Chappie had spun so many tales about his lineage that no one knew what to believe, her father knew he had spent several years living abroad. They had known each other through their fraternity, Sigma Alpha Epsilon, at the University of Georgia, but because

Chappie was three years behind him, her father had not really socialized with him.

When Julia called Chappie, he was most affable, immediately identifying her as her father's offspring, and inviting her to mid-morning coffee.

Chappie lived in a beautiful Georgian mansion on the West Harris Street side of Pulaski Square. Julia paused on the sidewalk and admired the beautifully maintained house and garden. Off to her left, above the rooftops of the surrounding houses, she could see the spire of St John's Episcopal Church. Not a bad location, she thought. Not bad at all.

Their meeting took place in the morning parlor. Chappie was dressed in a silk brocade smoking jacket with a pale lavender ascot at his throat. His butler, who had shown her in, was very Rudolph Valentino with his jet black, slicked back hair. The slight accent was icing on the cake, French perhaps. She wasn't sure. Chappie was more Truman Capote in his later years. The butler seemed to read her mind as she made the comparison. A wicked gleam appeared in his eyes and he quickly suppressed a grin as he left the room.

Chappie didn't disappoint. He spoke in a falsetto and held his pinkie high as he drank coffee from a beautiful Royal Doulton china cup.

"Now, my dear," he said, "what can I do to help you find the dahlin' Duke's royal rags?"

Julia took a sip of excellent coffee and smiled at Chappie. "As I told you on the phone, I've been hired to look into the theft. Peter Ryder spoke with you on Tuesday, I believe."

"Yes, yes, he did." Chappie made a face. "Very dour

man, all business. I tried to impress upon him the urgency of finding the royal apparel quickly. The exhibit is due to open in less than two weeks and a lot of expense has gone into constructing the display case and staging. These things require certain conditions, you know. Air temperature, light exposure, all sorts of things can damage the fragile fabric."

"How long have the arrangements for this particular element of the display been in place?"

"Strange you should ask." He favored her with a smile and a raised eyebrow not unlike her Aunt Ethel when she was gearing up to drop a titillating bit of gossip. "I got a call from the owner, Reginald Horchow, just three weeks ago. He had heard of the Russian Exhibition and wanted to offer the items to help round out the full historical impact of our little event." Chappie's lips formed a little moue. "His words, dahlin', not mine."

"Who made the arrangements?"

"Well, I did, of course. The museum is responsible for the care and handling of all the pieces in the display, hence the astronomical expense of the insurance." He offered up the coffee pot to refresh her cup, but Julia shook her head. "I did not, however, handle the transport details. That was all on Mr. Horchow." Chappie frowned. "In fact, he insisted on that aspect of the arrangements."

"Were you given the details of those arrangements?"

"Well, yes. After a fashion." He took a sip of his coffee then placed the cup on the marquetry table. "I thought it odd from the first. I mean, I had never heard of these people. I assumed it was someone he had done business with in the past and didn't think anything further about it." He sat back in his chair with a sigh. "Let's face it. I'm worn to the bone with this event. I can't be expected to micromanage every little detail, especially when the owner insists—and I do mean *insists*—on handling the delivery."

"Did Peter give you any hint of what he thought happened to the clothing, how it was stolen?"

Chappie's eyebrows lifted in a look of surprise. "Dear me, no. He was the most tightlipped man I've ever encountered. He wanted to come back the next day so I could look at some photos. It really wasn't a convenient time, so I asked if he could come back that same afternoon." He waved his hand in a dismissive gesture. "He wouldn't even accommodate me. Said he had an appointment at The Cloister and didn't know how late it might run."

"Who was he meeting? Did he say?"

"Well, really. The man is like a clam. He certainly didn't confide in me." He hesitated for a second. "But it wasn't about the stolen garments, I'm sure of that."

"How?"

"He said he had an appointment on another case and couldn't postpone it. The client was in town for only a few days."

Julia sat back in her chair and considered this. How did it figure into Ryder's disappearance?

Chapter Eight

Julia went directly to the Weatherby Insurance Agency after her interview with Alphonse Chapman. The weather had turned hot again as it often did in Savannah in September. By the time she walked to her destination she was happy to enter the air-conditioned comfort of the office.

Sandra looked up from her computer screen when Julia came through the door. "Well?" She was all smiles. "Tell me about your date. Isn't Doug divine?"

Julia smiled in return. "He's interesting."

"Interesting's good." Sandra leaned forward slightly in a conspiratorial posture. "So, you like him?"

She didn't want to get into a tete-à-tete with Sandra about Doug Heinz but decided to take advantage of the opportunity to learn more about him. Mitch's revelations of the previous evening had caused her to put the brakes on her enthusiasm for the hunky insurance salesman.

"How long have you known him?"

"Since he started working here last winter."

"Is that when he moved to Savannah?"

"He told me he was from Tampa." Sandra hesitated, a frown on her face. "You know, I just assumed he was new to town. I don't think he ever really said."

"Has he mentioned his family?"

Sandra shook her finger at Julia. "You like him." She grinned like the Cheshire cat. "You really like him."

Julia realized she would get nowhere with Sandra. The woman was clearly smitten with Doug. "I need to see Peter's files on the cases he assigned me. Are they on his desk?"

"Funny you should ask." Sandra's expression didn't look as if she thought it funny at all.

"Why's that?"

"Well, there's this U.S. Marshal…"

"Mitch Lawson."

Sandra let out a sigh. "Oh, good. You know about him."

"And?"

Sandra looked puzzled. "And he took the files."

Julia bit her tongue. "When?"

"This morning. He said he needed to review them and see if he could pick up Pete's trail."

Julia wanted to be angry, but Lawson was right. The best way to find Peter was to retrace his activities of Tuesday. "And you gave him everything?"

"Well, yeah." A look of doubt appeared in Sandra's eyes.

"What about his computer? Did Lawson take the computer?"

"No." Sandra stood and turned to the doorway to the inner offices of the company. "He should have a file on everything. That's how all the information about a claim originates and he prints out a copy." She paused in the doorway and looked around at Julia. "He's old-fashioned, you know. Can't break him of his old habits. Even keeps a dog-eared notebook where he writes all his thoughts and findings. If you can call it writing. More like hen scratches. Takes forever for him to transfer it to the computer file." Tears began to form in her eyes. "Hunt and peck." She turned from Julia. "That's our Pete." She drew a calming breath and with her back still to Julia said, "Something's happened to him, hasn't it? Something bad."

Julia placed a hand on Sandra's shoulder. She wanted to say something reassuring but suddenly realized her throat was too constricted to speak so she simply patted her on the shoulder.

"Right." Sandra opened the door to the claims department.

There at her desk sat Debbie, the claims secretary, her head only inches from Doug's as they consulted over something in a file. They looked up in unison as the door opened and Debbie quickly closed the file and placed her hand on top of it.

"Julia." Doug smiled and came around the desk. "What brings you here?"

She hesitated for a split second. "Work. I need to see Peter's files on the cases he assigned me."

"Oh. Sure." He glanced at Sandra. "But didn't Lawson take all the files?"

"Yes. But they should be on his hard drive as well." Sandra crossed the small anteroom and opened the door to Peter's office.

"Right." Doug's gaze skittered from Sandra to Debbie and finally settled on Julia. He gestured for her to precede him into Peter's office.

As Julia stepped past Debbie's desk, she glanced down and saw that the file she and Doug had been so engrossed in was no longer on her desktop. In fact, it was nowhere to be seen.

Peter had not secured his computer with a password. Julia was able to easily open all his files. She was acutely aware of Sandra and Doug hovering. She looked up at them. "I'm probably going to be a while. I don't want to keep you from whatever you were doing."

"Oh!" Sandra threw her hands up and turned for the door. "I left the front desk unmanned." Julia heard the anteroom door closing behind her.

Doug made no move to leave the office. Instead, he glanced through to the anteroom then crossed the office to close the door. He turned to Julia with a smile. "About tonight. We're still on for seven, right? Should I pick you up earlier?"

Julia sat back in Peter's desk chair and smiled at Doug. She didn't want to tip her hand that she suddenly had doubts about him. "I'm glad you mentioned tonight. I meant to call you earlier, but the day has been hectic." She sat forward, her arms folded on the desktop. "I have an appointment late this afternoon that puts me out past Ardsley Park. Why don't you meet me at The Club? I'll swing by my parents' house to change for the party."

Doug adjusted the knot in his tie. "Sure." He turned

toward the door then looked back at her. "Something to do with Peter's cases?"

"No." She smiled. "Personal business."

"Okay." He winked. "See you tonight."

* * *

Mitch sat with his feet on the edge of his desk, slouched in the chair, and the insurance agency's file folder on the Fechin theft in his lap. He heard Jones' feet hit the floor and the creak of Handel's chair as he stood. Mitch looked up from the folder to find Julia standing at his desk.

"Deputy Lawson."

"Ms. Hampton." He slid his feet from the desktop and angled his chair forward to face her. "What brings you to the courthouse this morning?"

"Peter Ryder's files."

"Ah." He cleared his throat but before he could say anything she cut him short.

"It didn't occur to you to tell me what you were planning? I could have saved you the trouble. As you know, I have a copy of the files on both cases."

"True. True." Mitch stood. "But I thought he might have made some notes on the originals. Or maybe there were things in there he hadn't shared."

"Why do you think he wouldn't share everything? It was his call to have me on the cases."

He motioned to the chair across from his desk, but Julia remained standing. Mitch sighed. "Look, the first rule of good detective work is to go to the original sources when you can. And I didn't tell you I was going to pick up the files because I didn't decide to do it until late last night." He paused. "After I left your place."

The telltale squeak of a desk chair caused Mitch to glare in the direction of Handel who had the good sense to look away.

Julia looked as if she was struggling with how she wanted to proceed. "Fine." She squared her shoulders. "So, what did you find? Any notes in the margins? Did you find the photographs?"

"Photographs?"

A pleased look spread over her face. "Yes, photographs. He was planning to return to Alphonse Chapman's house on Wednesday morning to show him some photographs."

"Of what?"

"I don't know."

"Huh." Mitch looked across the room and out the window, mentally filing away this tidbit of information. Julia cleared her throat and he brought his attention back to her. "What would you guess the photographs might be?"

"Off the top of my head, I would think they were taken of the missing items just before they were sealed away in the crates. It's standard procedure to establish a chain of responsibility. It's usually done by the authority in possession of the art just before shipment. They normally depict the item or items in place in the packaging materials but just prior to closing the crates." She shrugged. "A trail of breadcrumbs leading you through the process."

"And you think that's what he wanted to show Chapman?"

"I can't think of anything else it might be. Some art houses now do videos of the entire process to ensure the provenance of the pieces they ship. But Chappie said he had pictures."

"Chappie?"

"Alphonse Chapman."

"Uh huh."

"Well, what did you find?" Julia waited.

Mitch took his time responding. He hadn't found anything really. The files were exactly what the receptionist had told him they would be, a printout of the original claim. He cleared his throat again. "The only evidence that he even looked at the paperwork was one word on the inside of the file folder. I don't even know if it refers to this case. The file folder has been handled so much I think he must reuse it for each new case."

"May I?"

He handed her the folder and watched as she opened it to the inside cover. "Youngblood."

"Mean anything to you?"

"It's a name."

"I figured out that much."

"An old Savannah name."

"Yeah. I figured that out as well. There are hundreds of Youngbloods in the area." He pulled Handel's guest chair over and placed it beside his own. This time when he motioned for her to sit, Julia did. Mitch took the folder from her and opened it on the desk as he sat in his chair. "If you would, look through these and tell me if you see anything he didn't include in the papers he gave you."

Julia turned her attention to the folder just as the door to the agency flew open and banged against the wall. A blonde with big hair, short spandex skirt, and orangey-red lipstick marched across the room to Jones' desk.

"Bless her heart," Julia muttered to no one in particular.

Mitch looked from the blonde to Julia. "Why?"

"That lipstick, definitely not her color."

"I don't know," he sat back in the chair and looked the woman up and down. "It kinda goes with the rest of her."

"Exactly." Julia returned her attention to the file folder.

Mitch's eyebrows rose and he smiled. "Meow."

Julia lifted her gaze from the documents. "Hardly."

"If you say so." Mitch returned his focus to the documents Julia was passing to him one by one. He risked a sidelong glance in her direction. She was right. No competition there. She had that look that can't be acquired. Either you had it, or you didn't. Correct posture, simple but sophisticated hairstyle, flawless makeup, tailored clothing, and the rarest of all footwear; pretty, impractical, but somehow right.

In contrast, the woman who had entered the office was loud and getting louder by the minute.

"If you think you can palm me off that easily, you'd better think again." The blonde lifted her chin, hands on hips. "I know that snake is here." Her chest began to heave. "He can't do this to me!" She was on the verge of tears. "I saw his picture. It was him." She held up her left hand. "We're engaged," she wailed.

Mitch glanced over at the rapidly escalating scene and Jones jerked his head toward the doorway of the office. Mitch frowned as Jones jerked his head again. Handel coughed and said, "Pretty Boy," under his breath.

Julia was now openly watching the exchange. Mitch grabbed the folder, stuffed the documents into it and stood. "This isn't getting us anywhere." He held out his hand to Julia. "I think we should go back to the insurance agency and see what we can find on Ryder's computer."

Julia stood but shook her head. "Peter didn't operate

that way. He was old fashioned. There was nothing on his computer about either case other than the original claim application. And I checked his desk and file cabinet. No notes, no photos, nothing. But…"

Mitch took her by the arm and turned toward a rear door that led out of the office and down the back stairs. "But what?"

Julia frowned and looked down at his hand on her arm as he hustled her out the door. Once it closed behind them, he let her go and opened the door to the stairwell.

"What's going on?"

Mitch glanced toward the office door. "A delicate matter. Nothing to do with our cases."

He followed behind her down the stairs. The heels of her shoes tap-tapped with each tread. Some kind of purple-pink today, very plain but somehow the curve of the leather, the way it molded around her feet was sexy as hell. They somehow looked just right with the flirty pleated skirt. God, he loved a woman who wore skirts and dresses. And she wore them so well.

"So?"

"Humm?"

"Weren't you listening?"

"No notes, no photos."

"And?"

He had missed something. "And what?"

"Do you have any other ideas?"

Mitch hesitated a split second. "Nothing that relates to your cases." He looked along the street. "Which one's your car?"

Her eyes narrowed slightly. "I walked."

Mitch didn't want to chance Julia running into the

blonde screeching about Doug. "I'll walk you home." He really needed to get back upstairs and find out how one of Doug's women had found him, but first he had to get Julia away from the office.

"No thanks, Deputy Lawson. I'm going to the parking garage for my car. I have work to do."

"Such as?"

"A lead." With that she turned her back to him and started down the street.

Mitch fell into step with her after a couple of long strides. He needed to know what she had stumbled across. "So where are you headed?"

He could see she didn't want to tell him. Not out of a desire to thwart the investigation, he thought. Something else motivated her. "Look, a man's missing. Time isn't our friend. Do you really want to play cloak and dagger?"

Julia didn't respond immediately. Finally, she said, "Peter had an appointment at The Cloister the afternoon he disappeared."

"Who with?"

"Chappie didn't know. Only that Peter couldn't bring the photos back by that afternoon because of this appointment. The client was only in town for the day."

"Huh." They walked in silence for another block. "Was this the missed appointment?"

"I don't know but it would seem logical. Doug saw him just before lunch, so we know he didn't go straight from his meeting with Chappie."

"Doug saw him." Mitch frowned. "At the office?"

"Yes…" Julia hesitated. "I don't know. I just assumed it was at the office. At the time no one was really worried about him being missing and it didn't occur to me to ask where he had seen him."

"The appointment he missed, do we know who that was with?"

"It was about something entirely different. A six-month-old case if I were to guess. Items missing from an estate just prior to the auction."

"Who was in charge of the auction?"

"Sotheby's."

Mitch whistled softly through his teeth. "That kind of auction."

Julia nodded. "That kind of auction."

"Any Russian art among the missing items?"

"No. I have a copy of the file. Peter slipped it in with the two other files on the clothing and the Fechin. The stolen items were mainly expensive jewelry."

They walked around the corner and entered the parking garage. Julia stopped beside a classic Grand Wagoneer, its wooden panels gleaming, the paint pristine, and dug into her purse for the key.

"Great car."

She looked up at him and smiled. "Five hundred thousand plus miles. The odometer broke during my last year of grad school."

Mitch thought of Doug's expensive sport car. "You into classic cars?"

"Not particularly. My grandmother gave it to me when I turned sixteen." She slid behind the steering wheel and reached across to unlock the passenger door.

Mitch got in and ran his hand across the expansive front seat. The car might be a thirty-year-old everyman American car, but the leather was as supple as any new high-end luxury automobile made today.

They took the interstate and made good time. When they pulled up in front of the entrance to The Cloister, two uniform-clad young men whisked around the car and opened the doors.

"Good morning, Miss Hampton." The one on the driver's side smiled broadly as he handed her out of the car. "Will you be staying long?"

"No, Scotty. Park it close by, please."

Mitch watched this exchange then let his gaze roam over the structure before them before returning to Julia.

She could see the speculative look in his eyes and she suppressed a sigh. For once, just once, she would like to be known as Julia. Plain, ordinary Julia, not Julia Hampton; not The Bank of Savannah, Julia Hampton; not the great-granddaughter of Richmond Mercer, Julia Hampton.

She pushed the thought aside and entered the foyer of The Cloister. They were ushered into Scott Steilen's office and he came around his desk to kiss Julia on each cheek and to shake hands with Mitch.

When she told him what they needed, he immediately called up the guest log and confirmed that a Youngblood had been a guest at the resort on the day in question. Tallulah Youngblood. That fit with Peter Ryder's scribblings on the file jacket. She arrived in the evening of the previous day, had a late meal in her suite and a massage the following morning. An SUV picked her up at ten and she was back and had lunch at the River Bar at one that afternoon. She checked out at four.

"She's the insured on the estate theft. I tried to reach her at the number in the claims file this morning, but her assistant says she's enroute to Milan. She left New York last night," Julia said. "There was no mention that she'd been in Savannah."

Mitch sat back in his chair and stared out the window at the immaculately landscaped grounds. "So, the assistant didn't say anything about an appointment with Ryder?"

"No. She did tell me Ms. Youngblood was upset about the robbery because some of the missing pieces weren't to be auctioned. They held sentimental value for the family."

"What were they?"

She shook her head. "The assistant didn't know."

Mitch sat in silence, his gaze once again on the view. "Where did she go while she was here? Do we know that?"

The manager shrugged. "I can't say. The car was privately arranged. Ms. Youngblood still has family in the area. Or she may have had other business, her lawyer, perhaps."

Chapter Nine

The manager escorted them to the entrance where the bellhop went sprinting to fetch Julia's car. He chatted with Julia about the charity golf tournament to take place at the resort in early October, inquired if she planned to make one of the foursomes, and held the car door for her as she slipped behind the wheel.

Mitch was torn between the need to deal with the breach in Doug's security and the desire to follow up on the trail of Peter Ryder's disappearance.

"That case file on Youngblood," he said. "It might be helpful to review it and see if any items suggest Ryder's disappearance is linked to it rather than the Russian art."

"I've looked and didn't see any connection, but a second pair of eyes might be helpful."

Mitch watched her as she drove. Her slender fingers gripped the steering wheel, the nails done in the palest blush of color. Her ridiculously feminine heels worked the clutch, gas, and brake pedals. His gaze traveled up sheer stockings on shapely legs to the hem of her skirt hiked up enough to make him look away.

"I need to get back to the office. I could drop by this evening and look through the file over dinner."

When she didn't respond immediately, he looked over at her. He could see her formulating a refusal.

"Tonight doesn't work for me." She glanced at him then back at the road. "I have this thing, a family thing."

"Okay." He felt his voice held the right level of indifference. "Maybe tomorrow."

"Sure."

He had her drop him at the courthouse and stood watching until her car turned the corner and disappeared from sight. Their ride into the city had become strained. He should never have suggested dinner. The idea clearly didn't appeal to the belle of Savannah.

Jones looked up when Mitch entered the office. He leaned back in his chair and laced his fingers behind his head and grinned. "Guess how Marisha found Pretty Boy."

Mitch dropped into his chair and ran a hand through his hair. "I'm all ears."

"Couples Connection."

Mitch stared across the room at him. "What?"

"A dating site. Couples Connection. Marisha," Jones sat forward in his chair, "saw his profile online."

Mitch closed his eyes and shook his head. "Where is she?"

"Interview room three."

Marisha was applying lipstick when Mitch opened the door, that same orangey shade that, according to Julia, was not her color. He had to agree.

Mitch placed a file on the table and sat opposite her. "Marisha." He opened the file. "I didn't recognize you with your new hair color."

Marisha touched the springy curls of her hair, smiled, then her fingers went briefly to her roots. "Am I supposed to know you?"

"No. But we have a mutual acquaintance." He paused. "Viktor Letov."

"Viktor." She slammed her hand on the table. "That snake. One day we're engaged," she raised her left hand, fingers splayed to reveal a sizeable diamond, "and the next he's gone. Poof!"

"So how did you find him?"

She sat back in her chair, crossed her arms and narrowed her eyes. "I already told the other cop. Who are you anyway?"

"An acquaintance, as I said."

"Acquaintance." Marisha watched him in silence for several seconds. "Viktor doesn't have acquaintances who are cops."

"And you came to the U.S. Marshals' office looking for him because…" Mitch's voice trailed off and he waited.

Finally, Marisha threw up her hands. "That one with the bald head. I saw him with Viktor in Tampa. He was on the street today, sitting at a sidewalk table at a coffee shop." She shrugged. "I followed him here."

"Why did you come to Savannah? Did Viktor get in touch with you?"

Her fury returned in a rush. "A year! Almost. Not one

word. I had people breathing down my neck, watching my every move." She looked away and blinked rapidly.

Mitch had no doubt that the search for Viktor had been very thorough and violent. "I still don't know why you thought you would find him here."

"Duh. The internet."

"Sorry?"

"His profile picture? Couples Connection?" Her lip trembled then she got angry all over again. "He thinks he can just walk out on me without a word and disappear while all his goon pals go nuts looking for him?" She shook her hair back from her face. "Well, I showed him."

"How, Marisha? How did you show him?"

Her look was one of pure malice. "The Ferrari. I saw it parked on the street." She stared into Mitch's eyes. "He won't be taking any *antique car enthusiast* for a ride in it now."

"So, you're the artist."

The corner of her mouth curled up in a half-smile. "I ran out of room but the message reads the same either way."

Mitch couldn't help but smile back.

Jones opened the door and motioned for Mitch to join him outside the room. They had the Couples Connection website up on the computer.

Mitch swore under his breath as he read Doug Heinz's profile. "We've got to disappear Pretty Boy. Again."

He looked up as Handel entered the office. "I've lost him." The deputy wiped the perspiration from his shiny pate. "He went into a high-end men's clothing store and never came out. The clerk said he picked up a tuxedo he purchased yesterday and wanted to go out the back where his car was parked."

Mitch stared at the computer screen and let this tidbit of information filter through his mental files. He glanced at Handel, then Jones. "All the usual places, boys."

"And you?" Jones asked as he unlocked his desk drawer to retrieve his gun.

"A hunch."

* * *

I'm not sure why Julia keeps showing me different dresses. They look pretty much the same to me. I suppose it matters to men. And it certainly matters to Julia. Such a fuss about nothing, if you ask me.

I do like the shimmery look of this one, though. It seems she's made a decision at last but now comes the difficult part. She's opened the safe to reveal row upon row of shoes. There are a few shiny baubles as well but mainly shoes. It seems odd to keep them in a safe but then it also seems odd to have so many pairs. I can see this will take some time, so I'll leave her to it and make a swing through the kitchen. Perhaps she'll take the hint.

Unfortunately, there isn't even a stale cracker crumb to be found so I return to the window ledge to catch the last rays of the setting sun and check the street for curiosities and villains. The street is quiet but here comes a familiar car. I do believe The Lawman is about to pay a visit. But, no, he is simply sitting in his car all the way at the end of the block. Curious.

From the exasperated sounds coming from Julia, I decide she isn't pleased with her appearance, but I can't see a thing wrong with the final result of her grooming and putting her hair up, then down, then up. The earrings catch the light and the dress sighs softly when she moves. She has narrowed her shoe choice to three pairs. All in all, a far less indecisive procedure than her usual morning routine.

The Lawman still sits in his car down the block and here comes a long black town car. It stops in front of the building. Julia's cell phone rings and she answers, says okay, and hangs up. She chews at her lower lip then picks the middle pair of shoes to slip her feet into before she heads for the apartment door. So, she isn't expecting The Lawman nor is he to be her escort for the evening, but he's up to something. I must hurry before the opportunity to discover what is lost.

Julia has either lowered the window more than usual or a diet of Roquefort cheeseburgers and sushi is having an adverse effect on my physique. I barely squeeze through the opening, race along the molding, slide down the canopy, and drop to the garden wall before Julia settles into the backseat of the town car. It's a sprint to The Lawman's car but I make it just as he starts the motor. With one powerful spring from my hind legs, I leap through the open window of the automobile before he pulls away from the curb.

"Now, wait a minute," *he says.* "You're not going with me."

He reaches across the seat to grip me by the scruff of my neck and I jump into the back and out of reach.

"Damn cat," *he says under his breath as he pulls out into the street and follows after the town car.*

There's no reason for profanity, but I'll allow him this one slip-up. Besides, I need him and his car to see what's going on with Julia. Clearly, it's something that could put her at risk or The Lawman wouldn't be acting in such a secretive manner. I do believe he has fallen under her spell. Not hard to understand, of course, as she's a beautiful specimen of a female and quite charming. She puts me in mind of the lovely Veronica. The memory of which makes my heart rev up a notch. I can almost hear the sound of her sexy purr even now, all these months later.

But enough about all that, I need to focus if I'm going to figure out what has brought The Lawman to Julia's door. The break-in is at the heart of the matter, of that, I'm sure. My instincts tell me her work has drawn her into something bigger and more dangerous than art theft. The Lawman knows this. That's why he suddenly appeared on the scene. I need to discover what's really going on.

We quickly leave the historic district behind and soon come upon what looks like acres of well-tended green lawn on our right. The town car turns into a drive marked by gas lanterns and stops in front of a one-story brick building with a chimney on either end. Its squared up simple look is a bit of all right. There's a sort of high porch roof that extends over the roadway at the entrance. A young man in a gold braided get-up emerges to help Julia from the automobile. All very swank, I have to say.

The Lawman seems in a quandary about how to approach the situation. He sits with his car motor idling until Julia disappears inside and the town car pulls away from the entrance. He follows the town car to a parking area, parks, and looks in the rearview mirror at me. I can see him coming to a decision and I'm sure I won't like it. But, like it or not, I'll be ready for action at the first opportunity.

He lets up the windows of the car to mere slits and opens his door. Before he can get free of the vehicle, I dash over the seatback, out the open door, and across the parking lot toward the building. My keen hearing picks up another obscenity or two from The Lawman, but I don't hear any reference to 'that darn cat' so I decide to ignore it. There's a mystery right under my nose and I'm just the cat to solve it.

Chapter Ten

Mitch dismissed all thoughts of the cat as soon as he was out of sight. Callahan would either turn up or not. It wasn't a matter high on his list of concerns at the moment. Julia was all decked out in a heart-stopping gown and Doug Heinz had purchased a penguin suit. It didn't take an Einstein to figure out the two of them would end up at the same place at the same time. The problem, as he saw it, was how to extract Doug from the swanky Savannah Golf Club without creating a scene.

He decided a reconnoiter of the premises was in order. Only a fool walked into a hostile situation without knowing his options.

A turn to the right took him to the rear of the club. From there, a view of the golf course opened up and the rise and fall of berms constructed during the Civil War created a nice setting landscaped in lush green, fading into twilight. There were tennis courts off to one side of the building, and a veranda invited guests to take advantage of the rocking chairs and enjoy a beverage.

Mitch found the swimming pool. It was empty of swimmers in the gloaming of the day. Multiple doors opened into the main building. He returned to the veranda. It seemed the easiest and most logical point of entry for an uninvited guest.

An older woman stood on the veranda; the tip of her cigarette glowed in the fading light. Mitch could feel her gaze on him as he mounted the steps. He continued as if he had every right to be there.

"I guess someone forgot to tell you it was black tie."

She had a deep voice, a voice that didn't match her diminutive stature or her extreme thinness.

"I guess not."

She chuckled. "It's been a long time since a handsome young man crashed one of Woodrow's stuffy parties." She linked her arm with his. "Well, come on then. I suppose it's Julia you're after."

"Julia?"

"My niece. I'm Ethel Hampton."

"I'm pleased to meet you, Mrs. Hampton."

"Miss Hampton, much to my great-nephew's chagrin."

Mitch wasn't sure how to respond to that, so he asked, "What's the occasion?"

"Ritual scalp taking."

"Interesting."

"Boring. Until now." She led him through the open French doors and turned off the wide hallway into a good-sized room.

Waiters in white jackets passed among the guests with trays of champagne in cut glass flutes and tidbits of food that looked like works of art. Several groups of older men stood around looking bored as they exchanged desultory comments. The women tended to gather in small clusters with an occasional man thrown into the mix. One group of men was more animated than the others and at its center was Doug Heinz.

Mitch's companion followed his gaze and grunted. "Julia's friend."

An attractive woman crossed the room to join them. By the look of her Mitch knew she had to be Julia's mother. "Ethel," she said, "I don't believe I've met your guest."

"I found him wandering the grounds. Lost, I suppose. I invited him to join me as my escort." There was a wicked twinkle in her eye. "You don't mind do you, Audrey?"

"Of course not." She extended her hand as her eyebrows arched in question, "Mr. ..."

"Lawson. Mitchell Lawson." He shook the extended hand and noted that she didn't bat an eye at Ethel's explanation of him or at his attire.

Audrey was about to say something more when a burst of laughter came from the men conversing with Doug. At the same time a tall blond man, impeccably dressed in an expensive and well-tailored tuxedo, came up behind Julia and swung her around a couple of times to the music of a three-piece orchestra playing in the background. The two women Julia had been chatting with tittered with laughter.

"Well done, Audrey. Well done." Ethel Hampton took a glass of champagne from a passing waiter. She chuckled. "I didn't know you had it in you."

"I don't know what you mean, Ethel."

"Vinnie Richlieu, of all people. That would light a fire under anyone." Ethel took a sip of her champagne. "Although I don't remember him looking anything like *that*."

"Really, Ethel."

Mitch watched Julia dancing with Vinnie until the musicians came to the end of the piece. He forced his gaze away from the couple and let it drift over the other guests. He became aware of a squat but handsome man with white wings streaking through his dark hair staring intently at Julia.

"Who's that?" He asked with a nod in the man's direction.

"That's Rocco Sullivan," Audrey said. "He's an art dealer here in Savannah."

Aunt Ethel sniffed. "Art dealer, huh. If you take a wide view of what constitutes art."

"Oh?" Mitch realized Rocco Sullivan hadn't taken his eyes off Julia.

"Well, let's just say that if you purchased anything from him, it wouldn't be a bad idea to have it appraised."

"Don't stir that pot, Ethel. It's the kind of thing that can happen to any dealer. Pei-Shen Qian fooled thousands of people with his forgeries."

"Well, he didn't fool Julia."

At that moment a late middle-aged man joined Mitch and the two women. He extended his hand. "Woodrow Hampton." Unlike the women, his gaze did travel briefly over Mitch's long frame taking in his sports coat, lack of a tie, and boots.

Mitch shook hands. "Mitch Lawson, U.S. Deputy Marshal."

"Indeed," Woodrow said. All eyes in his little group were now on Mitch.

"I've been working with Julia. On a case. Missing art."

The wicked gleam was back in Ethel's eyes. "Really good show, Audrey."

This time Mitch thought he detected the shadow of a smile pass fleetingly across Audrey Hampton's lips. He turned his attention back to Julia and Vinnie Richlieu. This had to be the chosen one, Mitch thought. The socially acceptable, moneyed, and well-connected candidate for Julia's future husband. The family "thing" was really an occasion to show up the competition as lacking in every respect by comparison, to gently nudge her in the right direction.

Fine by him. He was here to do a job. Doug Heinz was about to disappear and once he did, Mitch was pretty sure neither of them would see Julia again. He watched Julia laughing at whatever Vinnie Richlieu had said and turned to scour the room for Doug. Time to put the belle of Savannah out of his mind and get on with the job.

Mitch nodded at the small group of Hamptons and said, "Excuse me."

He started across the room to where Doug was holding court. Suddenly a slender arm linked with his and he looked down into Julia's smiling face.

"Deputy Lawson, I'm glad you could join us."

"Are you, now?" The corner of his mouth lifted with pleasure.

"So, who are you following tonight? Me or Doug?"

"Tonight," Mitch allowed his gaze to travel from her upswept hair to the toe of the elegant little shoe peaking from beneath the hem of her dress, "you have my full attention."

He liked the way she blushed and the enticing sparkle in her eyes.

She drew closer to his side and lowered her voice. "Come meet Chappie. He's very entertaining and he loves an audience. We might learn something useful."

"Uh huh," he said, but he simply stood there staring down at her.

Julia's blush deepened and she tugged at his arm. "Come on."

The group around Doug consisted of three other men. Mitch had Chappie pegged even before the formal introductions. Also in the group was a man named Trip Youngblood. The name caught Mitch's attention.

"Mr. Youngblood." They shook hands. "That's a familiar name."

"Yes. I'm afraid there are more of us in the county than I can keep up with." He had that old money look and manners; nothing ostentatious, soft spoken, his white mane of hair just a touch long on the collar of his shirt.

Chappie chimed in. "Trip is being much too modest, Deputy Lawson." His gaze traveled up and down Mitch with open appreciation. "The Youngbloods have been in Savannah since Oglethorpe. They know where all the bodies are buried, so to speak."

"I'm not looking for bodies tonight, Mr. Chapman." Mitch caught Doug's eye. "Maybe another day."

Doug straightened his bowtie and turned his attention to Julia. "You look absolutely stunning tonight."

Julia performed a mock curtsey. "And you don't look half bad yourself."

"Indeed." Trip Youngblood said. "Mr. Heinz is quite the sharp dressed man tonight. He was just telling us a fascinating tale about his watch."

"Oh?" Mitch glanced down at Julia, then at Doug. "What's so special about your watch, Doug?"

Doug shrugged. "Nothing you'd be interested in, Mitch."

"Well, I'm interested." Julia smiled at Doug. "Let me see it."

Doug hesitated then shot back the sleeve of his tuxedo jacket as he glared at Mitch.

The watch was an exquisite antique timepiece.

"Rolex," Mitch said. "Wow. The insurance business must pay better than I thought."

"It's a family heirloom." Trip interjected. "Isn't it, Mr. Heinz?"

Doug's expression turned wary. "My great-grandfather's."

"Tell them the story, Mr. Heinz." Trip Youngblood glanced from Doug to Mitch then back again. "I'm sure they'll find it as fascinating as we did."

Julia linked her arm with Doug's. "Do tell, Doug. You've piqued my curiosity."

"Not much to tell. My great-grandfather took it off a dead German during World War II." Doug was looking more and more uncomfortable.

"Go on, man," Trip said, "tell them how he took it off the corpse of a German soldier at the battle of El Alamein. How he passed it on to his only great-grandson." He leaned back on his heels and eyed Doug for a long moment.

Mitch wondered what had set Trip Youngblood off about the watch. Was it merely that he had Doug down for the interloper he was, or was there more to it than met the eye?

Doug cleared his throat and adjusted the sleeve of his jacket. Suddenly, a streak of grey fury flew across the room from the open doorway and, with a twisting leap into the air, caught Doug by the sleeve. Doug let out a yelp and jerked back as glass from the crystal chandelier just above and slightly behind them shattered. Callahan fell to the floor and landed on all fours. Mitch tackled Julia and covered her with his body.

"I've been cut!" Chappie cried out as he stared at his hand where he had wiped at his face. "I'm bleeding!

"Get down!" Mitch yelled. He eased off Julia and checked her face, shoulders, and arms. "Are you hit?"

"What happened?"

"Are you hurt?"

"No. I don't think so."

"Stay down." Mitch rose to a crouch and pulled his gun from his shoulder holster. He duck-walked to the window and moved to the edge before he stood and glimpsed around the opening.

"Kill the lights, for God's sake!"

Chapter Eleven

*H*umans. *The old geezer was trying to tell them that The Voice,*
a/k/a, Doug Heinz, was a nasty piece of business but no one
would follow his lead. Now the burglar is gone, vanished in the hue
and cry over the gunshot. But I got my claws into him good. He'll have
a scar on that wrist, mark my words. It'll match the one on his left
calf perfectly if I'm not terribly mistaken.

The place is crawling with cops from the local police to U.S.
Marshals Deputies and the FBI. The Lawman doesn't seem to be
faring too well with Julia. She has rightly taken exception to the
fact he kept her in the dark about the true nature of The Voice, a
Russian mobster, and, I suspect, the one The Lawman calls Pretty
Boy.

It's a good thing I hitched a ride with The Lawman. Otherwise,
someone would be dead on this lovely Persian carpet. I suspect The

Voice was the target of the assassin's bullet, but I'm not one to jump to conclusions. That Chappie fellow begs a closer look. The bullet only grazed his cheek and he all but fainted when he realized what had happened. I doubt an ambulance was necessary to take him to the hospital for such a little scratch, but the hysterics were annoying.

The heat of the moment is over and, I must say, everyone, with the exception of Chappie, has taken the events of the evening in stride. I suppose the truly rich don't cower at the first sign of anarchy. If anything, the excitement has spiced up the party. Maybe they view it as something of a parlor game; the butler in the library with a candlestick.

I like Aunt Ethel. She has magic fingers and a sense of humor. Now if I could only hear what Julia and The Lawman are saying. From the body language the very polite, public exchange is anything but. From the smoldering look in The Lawman's eyes I'd say he's frustrated with the turn of events and, having seen him react to the fawning concern of Vinnie in regard to our Julia, he's also jealous.

"Looks like a lodge meeting," *Aunt Ethel says.*

"What on earth are you talking about?" *Julia's mother seems pleased with herself, but the comment causes little lines to appear on her forehead as she frowns.*

"A saying of Daddy's."

"About?"

"You remember Jeter?" *Aunt Ethel waves her hand dismissively.* "Of course, you don't. That was my childhood." *She runs her fingers under my chin and I almost lose the thread of the conversation.*

"Anyway, Jeter would disappear for days, sometimes weeks. Then he'd come dragging home, his fur matted, ear all torn, limping, and half starved." *She chuckles.* "Daddy would say he'd been to a lodge meeting."

"Honestly, Ethel."

"Well, just look at them, all bowed up." *She lifts me higher and rubs her cheek against my fur.* "That's what you wanted, wasn't it? To nudge Julia back out there?"

Julia's mother sighs. "She's twenty-eight. If she doesn't date, she can't find anyone."

"You should let her be, Audrey. She'll find the right one in her own good time. Or not. Marital bliss is overrated if you ask me."

"No one asked you, Ethel. I want grandchildren."

Both women are silent as their gazes travel from Vinnie to The Lawman.

"My money's on the deputy," *Aunt Ethel says as she scratches between my ears.*

Audrey frowns. "Really? Not Vincent or the guy who was her date?"

"I remember Vincent when he was Vinnie. And there's something off about the salesman."

"He's an insurance agent."

"Yes," *Aunt Ethel says,* "and he's selling himself all the time."

"Who do you think they were shooting at?"

Aunt Ethel chuckles. "My bet would be Chappie. He's the most annoying little piss ant."

"You're being ridiculous, Ethel. I'm sure they'll find it's some disgruntled former employee, or one of those little anarchists popping up all over the place these days, looking for attention, wanting to cause trouble for its own sake." *She sighs.* "Here in sleepy little Savannah."

* * *

Mitch's heart still raced. He had little doubt that Doug had been the target of the shot fired into the midst of the partiers. Julia had been standing at Doug's side, so close that the least tremor of the shooters hand, a minuscule change in the breeze, a moment of hesitation, could have caused the bullet to find Julia. He chastised himself for the hundredth time. What kind of lawman put the innocent in danger's way? And all in aid of a lowlife like Viktor Letov.

The golf course was alight with men searching for clues. They found the berm where the shooter had lain in wait for his opportunity. It was a professional job, no question about that. Mitch considered that an affirmation of his belief that Letov had been the intended target.

Although Julia's mother and Aunt Ethel seemed calm enough in the face of events, her father wasn't best pleased. He had demanded to know what was going on and in light of the need for a whole army of law enforcement personnel, Mitch had informed him and Julia of the true nature of Doug Heinz' sojourn in Savannah. It had taken a good deal of sweet talking on Julia's part to assure her father that Peter Ryder had brought her into this circle of danger by assigning her the cases of art theft. But Mitch knew Woodrow Hampton laid the blame squarely at his feet, and rightly so.

Though she had defended his actions to her father, Julia wasn't so ready to let him off the hook. "You should have told me."

"I couldn't."

"You couldn't?"

"He's a witness. It's my job."

She looked stunned for a moment. "Right. I see."

The teasing, conspiring cohort of earlier in the evening was gone. Mitch could see the change. It was there in her eyes, in her posture, in the bland smile.

"Well, Deputy Lawson, what happens next?"

"We'll find him. He'll disappear into a new life."

"I see." She stared at him a second longer. "And what about the thefts? What about Peter Ryder?"

"You need to let go of all that, Julia. For your own sake. It's too dangerous to pursue it any further." He could see her drawing away even though she hadn't moved. "These things will be resolved by the proper authorities."

"I see." She offered her hand. "Thank you, Deputy."

Mitch took her hand and refused to let it go when she would withdraw from the handshake. "Don't be foolish, Julia."

"I won't, Mitch." She managed to free her hand. "Not again."

Her father appeared at her side just then. "Come on, Julia. The car is here. You're going home with me and your mother."

Julia made no attempt at placating her father this time. "No, Daddy. I'm going home, to my home."

"You can't be serious!" Her father's face began to redden. "There's a criminal out there," he shot Mitch a scathing look, "who has designs on you."

"Don't worry, Mr. Hampton," Mitch said. "I already have two men posted at Julia's house and she'll be under my personal protection until we have our man in custody."

"Forgive me if I don't find that reassuring, Deputy Lawson." Woodrow Hampton was gearing up to do battle. "But I think I know best how to take care of my family. Julia is going home with me."

"Stop it, both of you." Julia took a step back. "I won't be imprisoned by your concern. It's my life and I'll live it as I like, doing what I enjoy."

Her father was on the point of exploding and Mitch raised a placating hand. "Don't worry, Mr. Hampton. I assure you now that we know the danger to Ms. Hampton, we'll ensure her safety." He was watching Julia as he spoke. "She has done nothing wrong and I'm going to fix this. It's my job."

Julia's eyes widened. "I won't have—"

"You have no choice. Until Viktor Letov is in custody, you're under protection from the U.S. Marshals. Whether you want it or not." His tone of voice brooked no argument.

"Of all the high-handed, manipulative—"

"Julia," Woodrow Hampton cleared his throat, "I think the deputy is right. If I know you, and I do, you'll be up to your neck meddling in this matter until you get yourself hurt."

"Meddling! You think what I do is meddling?" Her body was taunt with outrage. She looked from one to the other. "I won't stand for it, you hear me? I won't!"

With that she turned and stormed toward the door.

Woodrow Hampton gave Mitch an assessing look. "I'm trusting you with the only thing in my life I truly care about. You'd better keep her safe."

"Don't worry. I won't let her out of my sight." He shook Woodrow Hampton's hand and followed after Julia. For all his reassurances to her father, Mitch felt a niggle of apprehension. There was more to this woman than a charming Southern belle. She was intelligent, intuitive, tenacious, and rapidly becoming a pain in the butt. A charming pain, but a pain nonetheless. He needed to be spearheading the search for Viktor Letov but he found his concern for Julia's safety more compelling than doing his sworn duty.

He caught up with her as she descended the steps of The Club and slipped her arm through his. "This way."

"I have a car."

"Yes, I'm aware of that but you're riding with me. And dining with me, and sleeping—"

She tugged to free her arm from his grasp.

"—under the same roof as me."

"Of all the overbearing, chauvinistic—"

He stopped and turned her to face him. "Julia," he said, "shut up." Then he kissed her.

Chapter Twelve

The kiss caught Julia by surprise as did her reaction to it. She had always dismissed the notion of a kiss making a woman swoon, but she realized that it was a very real thing. Her knees went weak and her arms went around his neck even as her anger made her lean away from the kiss.

Mitch pulled her closer and said, "Stop it, Julia, or I'll be forced to kiss you again."

She squirmed to break his embrace and he was true to his word. He kissed her very thoroughly. This time she relented and let him take his own sweet time. When he finally broke off the kiss, they were both a little breathless.

He grinned down at her, and she smiled up at him.

"Well, Deputy Lawson, is this how law enforcement brings reluctant criminals to heel?"

"Are you reluctant, Miss Hampton?"

"Maybe you should do that one more time, just to make sure."

The arrival of Aunt Ethel bearing Callahan in her arms brought an end to the subduing techniques as practiced by one very handsome, sexy lawman.

Aunt Ethel tickled Callahan under his chin. "I was right." She sighed. "Too bad I'm not seventy years younger. I like a take-charge kind of man and I'd give Julia a run for her money over this one."

Callahan kissed Aunt Ethel on her cheek with his rough tongue and wriggled from her arms. He went to sit at Julia's feet. Mitch released Julia and scooped up the cat.

"Come on, you fur ball. I guess you'll have to be the chaperone." He took two steps up the stairs of the building to where Aunt Ethel stood and kissed her on the forehead. "Thanks for helping me crash the party."

Aunt Ethel patted him on the cheek and winked at Julia. "Go on, you two. And don't feed the cat. He's been stuffing himself on all those frou-frou tidbits Audrey insists on serving. I don't know why they can't serve real food. I'm going home and making myself a grilled cheese sandwich."

"Can we give you a lift, Aunt Ethel?" Julia thought it might be wise to have someone other than a cat as chaperone considering how she felt at the moment.

Aunt Ethel glanced from Julia to Mitch and gave them a knowing smile. "Not tonight. Regis is bringing the car around." As if on cue an ancient Rolls Royce rounded the curve of the driveway and crept to the entryway. The equally ancient driver got out and opened the back door for her.

* * *

The ride to Calhoun Square didn't take much time. They rode in a comfortable silence. Mitch felt mellow to his toes. He shouldn't, of course. Not only had he broken just about every rule of conduct of the U.S. Marshals Service when he changed the nature of his relationship with Julia, but Viktor Letov was out there somewhere. He should be with the small army of deputies and FBI agents checking all the usual places swamp scum gravitated to, in search of him.

Instead, he had assigned himself to the personal detail of Julia's bodyguard. It probably wasn't the wisest course of action considering how he felt about her, but he knew he couldn't let her out of his sight. Not because another deputy couldn't protect her, but because he would be useless at any other task; he had to know, to see with his own eyes, that she was safe.

The deputy posted to the front of her house was clearly visible. The goal was to make sure Viktor and any of his cronies knew she was well-guarded. He knew Jones would be watching the rear of the house just as closely and just as visibly.

The cat had been purring like a cement mixer from her lap for the duration of the ride. As Mitch pulled into a parking spot a few feet down from Julia's house, he stirred to life, stretched and yawned. He hopped out of the car as Mitch held the door for Julia and offered her his hand.

Her fragrance wafted around Mitch as he helped her from the car. They stood there, her hand in his, still caught up in that moment in time when danger didn't exist, the world faded away, and there was no thought of anyone or anything else. He wanted to kiss her again, could feel himself leaning in to do just that when the cat said, "Yeow."

Mitch sighed, grinned down at Julia, and looked at the cat waiting on the sidewalk, clearly impatient with their malingering. "I really didn't mean for him to take his job so seriously when I said he would be our chaperone."

"I think he may be concerned about your reputation with your co-workers." Julia glanced in the direction of the deputy leaning against the lamppost a few feet from her house. "Or do they already know your modus operandi?"

Mitch took her arm in his as they followed after the cat. "First of all, my co-workers pretty much know all my failings. Secondly, I don't have a modus operandi."

"Sure you do."

"Oh?"

"It's a mental thing. You stare into space, zone out, then come back to the moment."

"And how would you know that, even if it were true?"

Julia smiled. "I'm very observant. I studied art, remember."

"Uh huh." Mitch let that reminder fall into place. She was observant. If he was reading Aunt Ethel's comments correctly, Julia had exposed a forgery in a piece of art.

"See?"

"Hmmm?"

"Just now, that zoning out thing." Julia released his arm as they stopped before her front door. "It isn't very flattering to a girl who has just been kissed senseless."

"Senseless." He took her hand but didn't extract the house key from it. "I like the sound of that."

The cat began scratching at the door. Mitch took the keys from Julia's hand but instead of unlocking the door, he stood there, looking down at them. Callahan said, "Yeow."

"The watch." Mitch turned to Julia. "Did it strike you as odd that Youngblood wouldn't leave it alone?"

"He did seem a bit snarky about it."

"Snarky? Is that a word?"

Julia laughed. "In this case, yes. Trip is usually the most gracious man I know to everyone from the gardener to the mayor."

"That makes me think it was something about the watch."

"I tend to agree."

He opened the door and ushered Julia into the foyer. He locked the door behind them, checked it, and looked to see that his man was still alert. He went next to the office door, held up the keys so Julia could point out the correct one, then checked everything from the locks on the windows to the kneehole under her desk.

Julia trailed behind him up the stairs. He followed the same procedure in the apartment, first checking the kitchen then the living room. He frowned at the six-inch opening in the window. He closed it firmly and locked it.

When he turned toward the bedroom, Julia stood in the doorway, a look of misgiving on her face.

Mitch's brows arched in query and he watched as she chewed at her lower lip.

"You don't really need to check in there, do you?"

"I've seen your bedroom before, you know."

"Yes, well, it's just that I left things a bit untidy earlier."

He grinned. "Believe it or not, I've seen just about every type of ladies' apparel there is to see." He resisted the urge to kiss her again and moved her from the opening.

There were three dresses draped across the bed in a

haphazard fashion along with something lacy and sheer. He smiled in appreciation. Two pair of shoes looked forlorn, abandoned as they were in the middle of the floor.

Mitch checked the two bedroom windows and shook his head as he closed them and turned the locks. He decided Julia needed a lesson in how to be safe. A second story window was just as vulnerable as a ground floor window or door to a determined villain.

At the door to the closet, he surveyed the once neat room. Stockings draped over the ottoman along with a robe of a silky cream-colored fabric. The dressing table was cluttered with pretty pots and decanters and a scattering of jewels of varying types.

It was when Mitch turned his gaze toward the deep end of the closet that he was rendered speechless. Both of the doors to the safe stood open and his eyes traveled over row upon row of shoes; strappy strips of sandals, serious three-inch pumps in shades of the color spectrum Mitch had never imagined, boots of every description from low heel to high, cowboy to thigh high, rain to riding, and the icing on top—jeweled shoes from flats to heels, open and strappy, closed and beribboned.

He slowly became aware Julia was standing beside him. He glanced down at her then returned his gaze to the sight before him. "Well," he said, "there's bad news and there's good news."

"What?"

"Two pair tried to escape," he grinned, "but they only made it to the bedroom."

"Very funny."

"I do my best. This is a first for me. I don't think even Imelda Marcos had a safe for her shoes."

"I don't have a safe for my shoes. The safe was already here and I needed the space for my shoes."

"Well, then, that explains it."

"Explains what?"

"The break-in. They were looking for the combination to the safe."

"You were just getting back into my good graces. Do you really want to go down that road?" Her voice held a teasing note.

A thud followed by an impatient "yeow" from the other room interrupted what was definitely becoming something that would be hard to draw back from if it went any further. *That darn cat*, Mitch thought.

Both he and Julia took a deep breath then turned for the living room. Callahan sat on the desktop, a book and several files scattered on the floor below. When they continued to stand in the doorway and stare at him in consternation, he hopped down and pawed at the papers.

"What now, Dirty Harry?" Julia asked as she crossed the room to crouch beside him and lifted the top page.

Mitch knelt beside her and began sorting the pages according to name. An inventory of stolen items from the Youngblood case caught his eye. He dropped the other papers and stood. "The watch." He scanned the list of items on the page. "There's an antique Rolex listed on the claim form. And a note scribbled at the bottom of the page." He squinted and shook his head. "Maybe you can make it out," he said as he handed the sheet of paper to Julia.

Julia read down the list of items first then held the page closer and squinted. "Heirloom, I think, and WWII." She paled and handed the paper back to Mitch. "El Alamein."

She pulled out the desk chair and sat. "He was wearing the stolen watch." Her eyes were huge in her pale face. "Doug—Viktor." She scowled. "Whoever he is."

Mitch felt like he'd been kicked in the gut. The expression on Julia's face told him that she now fully understood the danger of her situation. Viktor Letov was a criminal, capable of nasty things, criminal things, and possibly, deadly things. That knowledge had shattered something in her, something innocent and trusting.

Julia rose to her feet. "We need to talk to Trip. Tallulah Youngblood is his niece. This watch must have been his grandfather's."

"Call him. I need to see him. Now. Tonight."

Julia picked up her cell phone and scrolled through her contacts, then dialed. After a minute she put the phone on speaker. The phone rang and rang. No one was answering at the Youngblood residence.

"Maybe he didn't go straight home. Do you have another number for him? A cell phone?"

She shook her head.

"Okay. Give me his address. I'll send a car ahead just in case." Mitch caught Julia by her upper arms. "You'll be fine here. No one will get past my men."

Julia pulled free of his hands. "It won't take me a minute to change. I'm going with you."

"No, Julia. Viktor isn't stupid. He's aware that his cover is blown. There's no way of knowing how he'll react." He could see her resistance building in her expression. "We could be walking into a dangerous situation."

She reached behind her and began to unzip her dress as she kicked off her shoes. "I can either go with you or I can follow after you. Your choice."

With that she turned toward the bedroom giving Mitch a fair view of the creamy flesh down her spine. It would have been erotic under different circumstances. Hell, it was erotic.

Chapter Thirteen

Julia was true to her word. In five minutes, she had stripped of her evening finery and reappeared in the living room in jeans and a turtleneck sweater, her hair pulled back in a loose ponytail. Mitch made one last appeal for her to stay behind but she refused to be persuaded. The realization of how easily she had allowed a ruthless criminal into her life frightened her. If she was going to overcome that fear, she knew she could not be cowed by the night's revelations.

When she left home for college it had taken a year for her to feel safe on her own. The love and concern of her parents, particularly her father, had left her fearful and fragile. It hadn't been their intention to make her apprehensive about the greater world but that had been the result of their solicitous concern throughout her life. The kidnapping and death of her father's cousin when the boys were children had marked him profoundly and though no one ever spoke of it, Julia knew that event kept him ever vigilant.

She looked across at Mitch and saw the set line of his jaw in the dim light from the car dashboard. He was furious with her, but she wouldn't be bullied by his concern. Her job, her self-worth, demanded that she see this thing through to the end. She clasped her hands together in her lap to keep them from shaking. A sense of dread had settled over her from the moment Trip failed to answer his phone. Something was terribly wrong. She felt it in her bones.

They raced toward Ardsley Park with the blue lights flashing. Although it seemed to Julia that it took far longer, the trip across the historic district to the south took a mere ten minutes at this late-night hour.

Two unmarked vehicles, their blue lights piercing the darkness, were already at the East 48th Street address when she and Mitch arrived.

"Nice digs," Mitch said as he held the car door for Julia. "Very Scarlett O'Hara."

Julia looked up at the beautiful white two-story house with its Ionic columns and graceful rounded second story balcony. She thought it one of the most beautiful houses in Savannah. Surely nothing sinister could happen in this fairy tale place.

They went up the wide steps leading from the sidewalk and along the front walkway to the house. As they stepped onto the porch, a plain-clothed officer came out the open front door. He looked from Mitch to Julia and stopped, partially blocking their entry to the house.

"Who's this?" He asked.

"Ms. Hampton, a friend of Mr. Youngblood's."

"She should wait outside," the officer said.

Mitch placed a hand on her shoulder. "Julia…"

"No." She took a deep breath. "He's all right, isn't he? Trip isn't hurt."

The officer looked from her to Mitch then back. He didn't say anything.

"He's not—he can't be dead." Julia felt a quaking begin deep inside.

The way the officer quickly averted his gaze told Julia that her fear had been realized. Trip Youngblood was dead. She looked up at Mitch. "I shouldn't have delayed you. If I hadn't insisted on coming with you, if you hadn't wasted time…"

"Stop it." Mitch glanced at the officer who got the message and disappeared back inside the house. "Whatever happened was already a fact when we tried to call. This has nothing to do with you."

"How can you know that? He might simply have not wanted to take a late-night call." Julia felt the internal shaking spread to her hands. She clenched them as she willed it to stop. If she fell apart Mitch would refuse to allow her into the house. She needed to see what had happened.

"This is a crime scene now, Julia. I can't allow you inside," he said as he waved a Savannah patrolman over.

She caught the lapels of his sports coat. "I can help." She closed her eyes for an instant and when she opened them, she had on her game face. "I know what to look for in the house, to see if anything is missing." She could read the refusal in his expression. "It might help determine what Viktor is thinking, what he might do next."

"This isn't something you should see, Julia." He held her by her upper arms. "I promise you, something like this will stay with you forever."

"I won't look at Trip." He was shaking his head at her. "I promise. Just at the room, the situation." She felt on the verge of tears and she knew she couldn't let that happen. "I need to do something to right this."

"This isn't your fault, Julia."

"It might not be my fault, but I can't help feeling that if I hadn't been so dense, if I had read the files more carefully, this could have been prevented." She tugged gently on his coat lapels. "Please, Mitch. Let me do what I can."

Mitch took a deep breath and released it slowly. "Your father is going to kill me."

"I won't let that happen."

Mitch waved the police officer away and together he and Julia entered the house.

The entry into the house was a twenty-five-foot-wide hallway with curved stairs on each side leading up to a second-floor landing about midway the depth of the house. Just past the righthand stairs, double doors opened into the library. The officer who had met them at the front door glanced up from his notebook. He shot a dark look in Mitch's direction. Another policeman was photographing everything in the room. Trip lay sprawled, face down, on the floor in front of a well-worn leather wing backed chair. A cut crystal highball glass had rolled about a foot from where he lay, a trail of liquid across the carpet marking its trajectory.

Julia averted her gaze from Trip's body. She didn't want to see how he had died. Instead, she started with the bookcases where he housed his antique book collection. Nothing seemed amiss there. Her gaze traveled on to the open areas within the paneled shelving designed to display paintings. She was looking for the Valentin Serov. The gallery lighting of the empty niche made its absence more profoundly obvious.

Here, then, was irrefutable proof that Viktor Letov was behind the theft of the other Russian art. Julia felt a rush of adrenaline, but she made herself focus and continued to mentally catalogue all the other items in the room. The Jan Brueghel the Younger pastoral was in its rightful place as was the portrait of a young woman thought to be the work of Rose-Adelaide Ducreux.

When she had made a circuit of the room, staying on the outer perimeter, well away from Trip Youngblood's lifeless body and the necessary things going on around it, Julia slipped out the door of the library and made her way to the kitchen.

Her hands shook as she filled the kettle with water and placed it on the burner to heat. Mitch came up behind her and placed his hands on her shoulders, pulling her gently against him.

"I shouldn't have put you through that." He held her there for a long moment.

The warmth of his body, the touch of his hands grounded her, comforted her. With a sigh she relaxed against him and drew from his strength until the kettle screamed. She busied herself with the tea preparation and found the ritual and his presence calming.

They sat at the battered, old table in an alcove of the kitchen. Julia wrapped her hands around the hot mug of tea, raised it to her face, and inhaled the steamy fragrance.

Mitch watched her in silence until she was ready to talk. He had a talent, she decided, with his quiet ways. It made you want to tell him things.

"There's a painting missing."

He didn't speak, allowing her to focus her mind and control her emotions. She stared into the amber depths of the tea as she spoke.

"It's a piece he acquired about a year ago. Nineteenth century Russian artist Valentin Serov. It was a painting of Peter the First."

"That would be Peter the Great?"

She nodded. "It wasn't one of his better works, quite possibly a cast off because of the quality, but it was a Serov and Trip was very proud of it."

She glanced up at Mitch and saw he was staring across the room at the crown molding around the ceiling, that pensive look on his face. After a moment his mind returned to the here and now and he looked at her hands still cupped around the mug of tea.

He took her hand and held it lightly in his. "You think it's related to the others, don't you?"

Julia nodded. "Yes."

"Why?"

"He took the Serov, I believe, because it's Russian. Other equally valuable paintings with better provenances were left behind. The Rose-Adeliade Ducreux is an especially fine example of her work. But he wasn't interested because she's a French artist."

"And you think Viktor did this."

She nodded again.

He stood and brought her to her feet with gentle pressure on her hand. "Come on. I'm taking you home."

This time she didn't protest. Though her hands no longer shook, she felt the shakiness inside, as if her internal organs were quaking with all she had seen and all she knew.

The guard at the front of her house had a reassuring effect and by the time they were securely ensconced in her apartment, Julia began to relax. The relief at being snug in her apartment with Callahan twining around her feet was like being drugged. She felt as if her legs could no longer support her.

Mitch obviously knew what to do. Without knowing how she got there, she was in bed, the comforter drawn up to her chin, and Callahan lay beside her kneading the covers and purring. His body, snugged against her, radiated warmth.

Chapter Fourteen

Mitch took the laptop from Jones and went back upstairs to the apartment where Julia slept. She had been in a state of near shock from the moment they discovered Trip Youngblood dead. By the time they returned to the apartment her body shut down, demanding that her mind escape into the balm of sleep until it could process what had happened and she could gain some distance from the night's events.

He looked in on her. The cat raised his head and eyed him through slits that glowed golden, before resting his head once again on her outflung arm.

Friday was now a memory, the night melting away into the early hours of Saturday. The security company had provided the Marshals with footage from Youngblood's house for the previous evening. They also had surveillance from the city camera on the corner across the street. Mitch logged into the laptop and pulled up the video.

At 10:10 p.m. Youngblood's Mercedes could be seen in the far-right corner of the recording as he pulled into his driveway. The wrought iron gates closed behind his car. There wasn't an angle from which the viewer could see what happened within the courtyard and garage but a few minutes later light from the library window fell across the paving stones just beyond the closed gate.

Mitch switched to the city camera to get a wider view of the street. At 10:22 p.m. a car appeared from the left and parked in front of the house. A man got out of the car dressed in what he assumed was a tuxedo because the white fabric of the man's shirt blazed in the low light when he turned to close the car door. Mitch paused the recording and enlarged the image. The definition wasn't great but he recognized the man as Rocco Sullivan.

The door to the house opened when Sullivan rang the bell. Mitch couldn't determine who had opened it because whoever it was remained in the shadow of the interior. He could only assume it was Youngblood.

At 11:01 p.m. the home security footage went dark. Mitch fast forwarded through a black screen until, at 11:39 p.m., the front view of the house reappeared with the strobing of blue lights. He switched to the city camera and saw Rocco Sullivan leaving the house at 11:09 p.m. Nothing else changed in the image until the first patrol car arrived at 11:27 p.m., not a shadow where there shouldn't be one, not a piece of trash blown along by the breeze, not a cat prowling the street. Nothing.

Mitch sat back in the chair and stared out the window

into the darkness of early morning. What was he missing? Finally, he stood and went to the bedroom doorway.

Julia slept restlessly, her hand twitched where it lay on top of the coverlet, her brow furrowed, she jerked her head to one side. She was very pale. Mitch felt remorse wash over him. And guilt. He had allowed this evil into her life and even when it was dealt with, the case finished, it would remain with her. It had forever changed her and there could be no going back.

He returned to the living room and found Julia's phone. He checked the call history and made a note of the time she had attempted to reach Trip Youngblood. If nothing else, he wanted to remove that doubt from her mind.

With his own phone he called the office. "Pull Gerty from whatever she's doing and send her over to the Hampton house. Round up Rocco Sullivan, the ex-fiancée, and the guy Viktor was seen with down by the river." He thought for a moment. "And the receptionist and claims secretary for The Weatherby Insurance Agency." He listened to the response from the other end of the call. "I don't care. Wake them up. I also want all you can dig up on Alphonse Chapman. He's a local." He closed the phone and slipped it into his pocket.

* * *

Mitch looked through the surveillance mirror into the interview room where Rocco Sullivan sat. At six o'clock in the morning he looked as well turned out as he had the previous evening at The Club.

With the timeline for the activities around Trip Youngblood's house late the preceding night firmly in his mind, Mitch entered the room.

"Mr. Sullivan." He placed his cup of coffee on the table and sat. "Would you like something to drink? Coffee, water?"

"No. Thank you."

"I appreciate your cooperation."

Rocco Sullivan gave a faint smile. "There wasn't much choice in the matter, but I'm happy to help, under the circumstances."

"And what circumstances are those?"

"Someone is going around shooting at the good citizens of Savannah. I imagine Chappie will be prostrate from this for a month."

"Yes," Mitch took a sip of his coffee. "From all indications he'll make a full recovery."

Rocco laughed. "You have to know Chappie, Deputy Lawson. He loves drama, real or imagined, and if there isn't any, well, he tends to stir the pot to create it."

"Really? So, you think he had a hand in this, what shall we call it? Escapade?"

"No. Chappie wouldn't go in for anything that involved real danger, especially if he's a potential casualty. His specialty is salacious gossip and innuendo."

"So, you have any ideas what this might be about? Who the target was?"

"Obviously it was one of the six people grouped together under the chandelier." He didn't smile but Mitch could tell from his eyes that he was enjoying himself. "That would appear to include four pillars of Savannah society, an insurance salesman, and," the smile returned, "a U.S. Marshals deputy."

"But you weren't far from the targeted spot."

"True, but if the marksman is that bad, well, we'll never know who he was trying to shoot."

"How well do you know the people in that circle, I mean, myself excluded, of course."

"I've lived here forty years, Deputy. I know all of them except the guy who works for Weatherby."

"Would you consider these people friends?"

Rocco shifted in his chair and angled his head slightly to one side. "Yes, for the most part. We all interact socially, belong to The Club, work for the good of the community. So, yes, I would."

"And Julia Hampton?"

"Ah. You've been listening to Ethel." He smiled. "I could see her bending your ear. She thinks I hold a grudge against Julia. I don't. It's in everyone's best interest to prevent fraud."

"Is that why you couldn't take your eyes off Julia all evening?"

"Jealous, Deputy Lawson?"

"What did you do after you left The Club?"

"Went home, checked my mail, checked my messages, and called Trip Youngblood."

"What about?"

"Is that really any concern of yours?"

"I'm afraid it is."

Rocco was silent for a long moment. "We had business to discuss. I'm an art dealer and I was doing some investigating for him."

"Investigating what?"

"The provenance of a painting he acquired some months ago."

"The Rose-Adelaide Ducreux?"

Rocco sat up straight in the chair. "How do you know that?"

"What did you do next?"

"I went over to Trip's house."

"Why?"

"To take him the report I found in my mail from Belgium. He was beside himself to establish the authenticity. We were able to track down a great-great-grandson of the original owner of the painting. He had old family photographs revealing the piece in the background."

"And this is proof enough?"

"It goes a long way in affirming everything we know so far. The painting has been thoroughly examined by three experts. All the elements are in keeping with the period. This is just further evidence in support of what we believe."

"So, what happened next?"

Rocco shrugged. "I gave him the file. He put it in his safe and I left."

"Nothing else happened when you were there?"

He frowned. "No. He answered the door when I got there. It was late. The staff had already gone to bed, I imagine. We went into the study. He was having a bourbon, offered me one but I declined. I wanted to get those documents in his hands and get back to an early bed."

Mitch stretched his feet under the table, leaned back in his chair with his fingers laced at his waist and waited.

"The power flickered. Right after I got there." Rocco seemed to be searching his memory. "That's it."

"How long were you at the Youngblood house?"

Rocco shrugged. "I don't know, maybe fifteen, twenty minutes."

"You're sure about that?"

"I didn't check the time, if that's what you're asking. I took the documents over. Trip read through them while I was there, so maybe I was there a few minutes longer, a few minutes less. I really don't know."

"How did Mr. Youngblood seem when you left him?"

"I'm not sure I know what you mean. He was happy enough to get the reports. There was a copy of two photographs from the great-great-grandson included in the documents. He took a moment to look at them with the magnifying glass before he locked everything away."

"So, he was alive when you left him?"

"Alive?" Rocco reared back in his chair. "What kind of question is that? Of course, he was alive."

"Not anymore."

* * *

Julia woke and sat straight up in bed. Callahan sat in the window looking out. He turned when she stirred from sleep and blinked slowly as if in greeting. She remembered the warmth of his body in the night, the gentle purring.

"Come here, you."

Callahan hopped down from the window ledge and leaped onto the bed. She pulled him close and tickled him under his chin and between his ears. "You're such a good kitty."

His ears flattened momentarily as if the diminutive endearment was insulting then he endured her caresses for a few minutes longer before he rose, hopped off the bed, and left the room. Julia became aware of the smell of coffee.

"Food," Julia said softly, "that's always foremost in

your thoughts." She threw back the comforter and slid out of bed. She padded barefoot through the apartment to the kitchen. There she came to an abrupt halt. A woman with fiery red hair, pulled back severely, stood at the island doctoring a cup of coffee.

"Good morning," the woman said. "I'm Gerty." She gave Julia a quick once over in assessment and took a sip of her coffee. "Mitch sent me."

"Why?"

"To keep an eye on you."

"Oh." Julia went to the cabinet and got a cup. "How long have you been here?"

"Since about four."

The clock on the wall read seven-thirty. "I overslept." The comment sounded absurd even to Julia's ears. How did you make conversation with an unexpected stranger in the middle of your kitchen first thing in the morning?

"You're allowed. You had a rough night."

The memories of the previous night came rushing back and Julia turned from the woman in the pretense of doctoring her coffee. She took a deep breath and realized she couldn't think about what had happened without her heart pounding and her hands shaking.

"He was a friend." She spoke to the tile backsplash, unable to look at the strange woman in her kitchen as she remembered Trip. "A dear man."

"That's tough," Gerty said. "Look, is there some place I can park to be out of your way?"

Julia turned to look at her unexpected guest.

"I know how it is in the morning," Gerty said. "I have my routine and I like the quiet. So, if you'll just tell me where I'll be the least intrusive, I'll get out from under your feet."

Suddenly Julia wanted very much to be alone. She needed to work, to sort through what she knew, and find the missing pieces. In the light of a new day, she knew she wasn't in danger. The break-in at her office had been in search of the file on the estate theft. Letov somehow discovered Peter Ryder had slipped it to her, and he had wanted to either destroy it or alter it. He was a thief. Whether or not he was a murderer was yet to be proven. But in either case, she wasn't a threat to him. He was already known to law enforcement; his new identity vanished last night when Trip saw through him. There was no way she could expose him or incriminate him. In her heart she knew Letov had no further use for her. It was a very freeing thought. The fear that had gripped her the night before was gone. Only sadness at the loss of a dear friend remained.

"Are the deputies still posted outside?"

"Sure."

Julia walked to the living room and looked out the window. The night had turned cool in the late hours and the man on duty had the collar of his jacket turned up, a stocking cap on his head, and his hands jammed in his pockets.

"I imagine they could use some coffee."

Gerty came to stand beside her. "Probably."

"Why don't you take them some while I get a shower?"

She hesitated. "I'm not supposed to leave you alone."

"Who's going to get in here with a deputy on the front door and one on the back?" Julia smiled. "It's not as if you're going anywhere."

Gerty was silent for a minute as she watched the guy on the front sidewalk stamp his feet. Julia could see her colleague's discomfort working on her.

"Okay." She turned toward the kitchen.

While Gerty prepared coffee for her fellow deputies, Julia returned to her room and began a quick, abbreviated version of her morning routine. She was in and out of the shower in record time. Dark jeans, boots, and a pullover sweater with a fleece vest over it and she was dressed for the day. A look in the mirror revealed dark smudges beneath her eyes but she didn't tarry with her makeup. A dash of mascara and a quick swipe of lipstick finished the job.

She was already sorting the files Callahan had pushed to the floor the previous evening when Gerty came back upstairs from chatting up the deputies stationed at the front and back of her house as she delivered their hot coffees. What Julia needed was in these notes somewhere, she was sure of it.

Once she had everything sorted, Julia settled on the sofa and began a methodical review of every document, note, and photograph. When she finished the Youngblood file, she knew without doubt her conclusions on the matter were true. Viktor Letov was somehow involved in the theft of over three-hundred-thousand-dollars worth of jewelry. Peter Ryder had known the history of the Rolex watch and jotted the key words in the margin of the file's pages. She now believed he had suspected Viktor Letov's involvement and had lumped it in with the missing Russian art cases so as not to alert Letov of his suspicions.

Julia knew from Mitch that Letov had been a money handler for elements of the Russian mafia. How did that tie in with the other two cases? If Letov was due to testify about the mafia's money schemes, would he then reach out to anyone from his past to traffic in stolen Russian art? It didn't seem likely.

Was Doug Heinz, a/k/a Viktor Letov, a cold-blooded

killer? Julia shivered at the thought she could have been so misguided in her assessment of him. She had known from the start that he was charming, intelligent, and she had sensed an element of danger. The realization that she had been attracted to that aspect of his personality shamed her. If she hadn't invited him to The Club, would Trip still be alive? Regardless of what Mitch said, she knew she had set this chain of events into motion. The only thing she could do now to right this grievous wrong was to find Trip's murderer.

Where to start? Julia glanced down at the open file in her lap. Perhaps the best place would be the Fine Art and Antiques Shipping Company and Renee Slovaska, Art Specialist.

Chapter Fifteen

Julia had done a cursory search into the shipping company when she was first assigned the file. It was a legitimate business, incorporated six years earlier. Their corporate offices were in Miami, but they also had a satellite office in the docks area in Savannah. Here, then, she thought, was a starting point.

Earlier in the investigation she had been distracted from a closer look at Renee Slovaska by the arrival on her doorstep of Mitchell Lawson. That lack of professionalism might have cost Trip Youngblood his life. And Peter Ryder was still missing. She fired up her laptop and entered Renee Slovaska's name.

After twenty minutes of searching, Julia still didn't know much about Slovaska. Her employment with the

Fine Art and Antiques Shipping Company began eighteen months earlier. She was listed in their roster of mid-level employees. She had transferred from the Miami office eight months ago. The fact that she had landed in Savannah at almost the same time as Doug Heinz wasn't lost on Julia. Also suspicious was the lack of a Facebook page, a paper trail beyond a LinkedIn profile, or any other social media.

Julia felt momentarily stumped. She read over her notes from her interview with Chappie. The owner of the historic apparel had arranged the delivery, had insisted on it, according to Chappie. She dug through the file and found Reginald Horchow's phone number.

A woman answered the phone when Julia called. She identified herself as Mr. Horchow's secretary and said that her employer was in the hospital, the result of a heart attack. There was very little she could tell Julia about the missing clothing of King Christian IX. She did remember her employer being elated that the garments were going to be part of a legitimate exhibition on Russian art and history, but she knew nothing of the arrangements.

Something kept niggling at the back of Julia's mind but whatever it was, she couldn't bring it forward.

Her next call was to Chappie. His butler answered the phone and informed Julia that Mr. Chapman had not yet risen from bed. The previous evening's events had taken their toll. Julia couldn't tell if the man was being flippant or if his accent only made it seem that way. She didn't hear a great deal of concern in the man's tone. Perhaps he was accustomed to Chappie's mercurial ups and downs of temperament.

Adoni, as he identified himself to Julia, couldn't help her with any information on the missing apparel. He handled Mr. Chapman's personal matters, he said, things like his social calendar, shopping, travel arrangements, household staff.

When she hung up, Julia decided she needed to pay a visit to the Fine Art and Antiques Shipping Company office. That was the only logical next step. But how was she going to slip away from her guard dogs? There would be little hope of learning anything of value if she arrived with an entourage of law enforcement personnel.

She got up from the sofa and looked out the window. A replacement deputy had arrived sometime in the past half hour and from what she could tell, he was in the process of interrogating her father.

She smiled and shook her head at the scene below. This treatment wasn't sitting well with her father.

He was bowed up with outrage, his face red, his arms rigid at his side. She tapped on the window.

Both men looked up and she gave a thumbs up sign to the deputy.

The first words out of his mouth when her father stormed through the apartment door were, "Did they tell you? About Trip?"

Gerty stood at the ready to engage her father, physically, if necessary, the instant he burst into the room.

"Yes, Daddy. This is Gerty." She gestured toward the deputy. "She's with the U.S. Marshals Service."

"Well, it's a hell of a poor job they're doing, if you ask me." He took off his hat and threw it onto the bombe chest in the foyer.

Gerty held her tongue and disappeared back into the kitchen as Julia gestured for her father to have a seat on the sofa.

From her father's comment it was obvious that he didn't yet know she had been at the scene of the murder in the early hours of the morning. It was in her best interest to keep that information from him as long as possible. The last thing she needed was for him to start insisting she relocate to Ardsley Park for the duration of the investigation.

Callahan came strolling into the room. He crossed to where her father sat and sniffed at his shoelaces.

Her father shooed him away. "Why, in heaven's name, did you agree to cat sit a stray cat? He could have a disease, or fleas, or God knows what."

Woodrow Hampton sneezed twice. Julia was suddenly struck by a solution to her semi-captivity.

At her father's words, Callahan turned his back on him and flattened his ears.

Julia scooped him up from the floor and sat in the armchair. "He's not such a bad guy," she said as she averted her gaze from her father's scrutiny and rubbed Callahan's ears. "And he's not a stray. He belongs to Dax. I have to take him to the vet this morning."

"Honestly? A murderer is running around Savannah killing everyone we know, and you want to take the handyman's cat to the vet?" Her father stood, sneezed again, and began pacing the room. "Of all the hair brained—"

"I know, I know." Julia dropped Callahan to the floor, surreptitiously grabbed her cell phone from the end table, and went through to her closet to get a pair of gloves and a scarf. She was zipping her fleece vest when she re-entered the living room.

"You need to stay put, Julia. It's not safe for you out there." Her father looked from his daughter to the cat. "And anyway, I don't see anything wrong with him."

At that moment Callahan looked up at Julia and sneezed.

"See?" Julia said. "And besides, I'm up to my eyeballs

in law enforcement. They won't let me so much as go downstairs to the office and work."

She gave her father a hug. "Besides, what could be more harmless than sitting in a vet's office while they see if he's really sick?"

Julia knew she was hitting all the right buttons. A trip to the vet would take her out of the loop of the investigation, place her in a neutral environment in a place she wasn't known to frequent. She could almost see the wheels turning in her father's mind.

She picked up the cat and started to the door. "Gerty, I'm taking Callahan to the vet."

Gerty was already slipping into her coat. She eyed Callahan then looked Julia in the eyes. "Okay. Let's go."

Julia knew that if she didn't put up a protest they would see through her sham. "Honestly, Gerty, it's just four blocks away. I don't need a babysitter."

Gerty shrugged and opened the apartment door. End of story.

Julia sighed. "Fine, but don't blame me for wasting the Marshals' time and resources. If Viktor Letov is the devious criminal you think he is, then he's long gone from Savannah."

* * *

I'm not sure what Julia has in mind. A trip to the vet isn't happening. But I feel her claustrophobia. Her apartment is like living in a pawn shop. There are so many guns, all on display as a show of force. A breath of fresh air will do us both good and blow out the cobwebs. The Lawman has us locked up as if an evil presence could slither through the slim openings in the windows. No one, excluding myself, of course, could accomplish that feat.

I appreciate The Lawman's concern. He's been charged with keeping Julia safe, but he has failed to take into consideration that I'm on the job. Wherever it is we're going, I'll be on the lookout. The sooner we resolve these thefts, the better for Julia. Though she doesn't come to sleuthing naturally like me, she's proving to be a very determined detective.

There's a definite chill in the air as we stride along, Gerty keeping pace, with one of the other deputies taking up the rear guard. I burrow into the warmth of Julia's vest. We'll see what unfolds.

I'm not happy to see cutesy paw prints on the glass door in front of us. That's a sure indication we're about to step into the realm of veterinary medicine. Julia is chatting up a freckled young woman behind the counter and I do my best to look pitiful.

"A cough, you say? That can be tricky. We'll listen to his lungs and check for a temperature. Come with me."

We're ushered through the door to the inner rooms of the clinic after Gerty is convinced, with only a minor standoff, to wait in reception.

But what is this coming my way in the arms of a man? Be still my beating heart. A beautiful mocha Persian femme fatale is being borne past me and the scent of her is intoxicating.

"Yeeeooooww." *She looks my way and blinks seductively. The ladies always give me the come-hither glance. I clamber up to look over Julia's shoulder, but she has me in a tight grip. I wish I didn't feel honor bound to remain on duty. Females in peril seem to have become my Achilles heel. The door closes as I watch, the saucy siren is lost from view. Pity.*

A side door opens, and we step inside to find a friendly ginger-headed Doctor laying out implements. This is not a good thing. I'm perfectly willing to go along with Julia's ruse up to a point. We've reached that point.

She smiles. "Ray Claiborne. Thank you for doing this but I just realized Callahan is fine as a fiddle. He's only been playing at being sick so I'll give him something other than cat food. Either that, or he's a bit of a hypochondriac."

"Don't you want me to check?"

The way Dr. Claiborne is looking at Julia leads me to believe that I could die a slow, painful death on this examination table and he wouldn't notice. I do believe she has all of Savannah under her spell.

"No, no," *she smiles and gives him a kiss on the cheek.* "I know you'd rather be spending your Saturday elsewhere. You're a doll for working us in ahead of everyone and I feel guilty about that. There's no need to make them wait while Callahan makes his play for attention."

Enough. She has taken this too far. It's one thing to use me as a method of escape but something altogether different to malign my character. I hiss and knead her arm just a little more forcefully than necessary.

"Callahan!" *She scratches my ear and gives it a less than affectionate tug. For the Doctor she maintains her smile.* "Thanks, Ray. Really. I'll see you at the Juan Diego Florez performance?"

"Sure," *he says as he follows us out into the hallway. It's obvious he's reluctant to see her go.* "Maybe we could have dinner beforehand." He blushes. "If you don't have plans already."

"That sounds lovely. I'll call you." *She hesitates.* "Umm, could I go out the back?" There's that smile again. "Someone I really don't want to get entangled with right now is in the waiting room."

The Doctor's eyebrows shoot up and he gives a small shrug. "Fine by me." *He gestures toward the rear of the building.* "This way."

And just like that we are out on the street again, not a flatfoot in sight.

At the corner Julia stuffs my head into the confines of her vest and lifts her hand in summons of a taxi. One pulls to the curb and we are off, exactly where, I've no idea until some ten minutes later the scent of the sea is heavy in the air. I peek my head out the zippered opening and see that I'm right. We're at the docks. The smell of diesel and salt air mingle with a distinct metallic odor. There are cargo containers stacked to the right and left of us and straight ahead I can see tankers lining the dockside and a glimpse of a high arching bridge to my left.

The taxi disappears from sight and Julia turns from the view of the docks and looks at the buildings just beyond the rows and rows of cargo containers. These metal constructions are a far cry from the beauty and grace of what I've seen of the city so far. They're functional and not much else. Julia makes a beeline to one with a battered door that was once red. The sun has faded it to the color of rust.

No one answers her knock. "It appears they aren't open for business on Saturday." *She tries the door and discovers it to be unlocked. As she pushes it open, I struggle free of the fleece vest and drop to the concrete floor of the building.*

"Callahan!" *Julia hisses at me.* "Come back here!"

I ignore this demand. I'm here to do a job and being snuggled in the comfort and warmth of her bosom, while not a bad thing, doesn't help solve the mystery of stolen Russian art and artifacts. There's a scent here I recognize. The Voice, Pretty Boy, or whatever he calls himself, has been here ahead of us.

We seem to be in some type of reception or office space. It's about six feet deep by ten feet wide. A counter, about three feet in length, forms a barrier of sorts. Behind it I find three tall file cabinets and a drop-down shelf that appears to serve as a desktop. It holds a laptop computer. I leap onto the pseudo desk and sniff the computer.

The screen is closed over the keyboard. There isn't much else on the desktop.

The space beneath the counter has some open shelves up high with cabinets below. I drop back to the floor and paw open one of the cabinet doors. It's filled with haphazardly stacked file folders that smell old. Nothing recent has happened here.

Julia is busy looking through a large ledger she took from one of the open shelves of the counter. From her expression I don't think she's having any more luck than I am. She turns to the laptop, lifts the screen, and fiddles with the keys. Nothing happens.

A door is situated a few steps along the rear wall. Julia opens it. I slip over to the open doorway and decide a look-see is in order. The scent of The Voice is very strong here.

The door opens onto a large storage area filled with crates and boxes of varying sizes. They rest are on pallets for easy movement by the behemoth yellow machine that sits quietly in one of the aisles formed by the crates. I hear Julia's footsteps behind me though she is doing an admirable job at being as quiet as it is possible for a human. A noise deep in the canyons of the mounds of boxed material reaches my ear. It's a voice, a voice that's known to me.

I'm off like a streak of light on silent paws. In seconds I've discovered the location of The Voice. He's with a woman and two men. They're standing outside an office that has been built out into the floor space of the cavernous building. It appears that none of them is happy. They speak in clipped tones and a language I don't understand. One of the men gestures aggressively. The Voice is still wearing his evening attire. It's much less impeccable than when I last saw him at The Club.

One of the men with him has a very nasty looking gun slung over his shoulder. This isn't the weapon of an amateur but rather something that Dax would know a thing or two about from his Army days. I'll need to be very cautious as I make my way around them to see what's in the office. There just might be a clue to the whereabouts of Peter Ryder. I've no doubt that Julia and I have stumbled onto an operation of the Russian mafia. If I had to guess, I'd bet they're speaking Russian and I fear Peter Ryder may have found himself on the bad side of them.

At least for the moment, they're focused on each other and whatever topic has angered the woman, which gives me my chance. I'm within an easy distance to the open office door. All it will take is a quick dash.

Suddenly there is a clatter that sounds like metal pipes bouncing against concrete. The sound echoes through the building. The four people outside the makeshift office spring instantly into motion. The Voice and the woman rush into the office and close the door. The two men fan out and head into the bowels of the building.

I know without doubt that it's Julia who made the noise and she's now in grave danger. I have to find her before these men do. My headlong rush to locate The Voice left her alone and vulnerable. My curiosity has put her in danger.

Chapter Sixteen

Julia found nothing in the outer office of the Fine Art and Antiques Shipping Company that suggested it was anything but a legitimate business. The ledger contained a log of ships, cargo manifests, and dates. The laptop was password protected which, in and of itself, wasn't suspicious, only good business practice. Almost as soon as she opened the door to the interior of the building, Callahan had taken off like a flash. Now Julia would have to find him.

The warehouse was filled with row upon row of merchandise. Their height served to diminish the scant light that filtered in from the dirty narrow windows along the walls up near the high ceiling of the building. Julia read the logos stamped on the wooden crates as she worked her way toward the center of the structure.

She became aware that she wasn't alone. There were faint voices coming from somewhere within the structure, but the sound was distorted and she couldn't determine the direction.

For a moment she stood still, trying to orient herself. She thought she knew where the door to the reception area was. Callahan had disappeared so quickly that he could be anywhere within the building. Her best bet, she decided, was to make her way to one wall and then follow it until she knew where she was and pray she found the cat before either of them were discovered trespassing.

When she reached the far wall, she could hear the voices more distinctly. She recognized the basics of the language as part of her study of Russian art and history. To know it was one thing, to follow a conversation was another. The rapid exchange only allowed her catch a few key words but she clearly heard a man say something about a watch, diamonds, and money.

Straining to follow the exchange more closely, she leaned around a pallet of crates to look down the corridor from which the voices came. Far down the building she could see the arm of a man who gestured as he spoke. She inched out a little farther and all heck broke loose. Her shoulder caught a lone metal pipe sticking out from a row of three-inch pipes stacked on top of some wooden crates. Helpless to stop the following cascade onto the cement floor, the clatter was deafening. The pounding of her heart was almost as loud.

The fight-or-flight response took over Julia's body and she ran from the chaotic scene and zig-zagged between the towers of crates. Her heart was beating rapidly and she was breathing heavily when she saw a small opening where excess pallets had been stacked on top of each other. Working her way between them, she fought to control the sound of her breathing. What was she to do now?

Footsteps sounded, passing nearby on the other side of the stack of pallets. Through the open woodwork she could see a man, a gun cradled in his arms. He stopped in the aisle and listened. Julia closed her eyes and said a silent prayer. When she opened them, the man was staring directly at her. She almost cried out in fright but quickly realized that although he stared in her direction, the low light and maze of the haphazardly stacked pallets shielded her from view.

Finally, the man moved on. Julia felt weak in the knees. What direction had he had taken? How many of them were there? She concentrated on the exchange she had overheard. At least two men and a woman, she decided. Okay, she knew at least one of the men had a gun and it was a very serious gun. She could only assume the other man was armed. Perhaps the woman was as well. She couldn't discount the possibility.

The first thing she had to do was figure a way out of the building. There was Callahan to worry about, but he was a smart cat. Surely, he would keep out of harm's way until she could return with help.

The thought of what Mitch would have to say about her little escapade made her cringe. He had been right. Between him and her father she was in for a real tongue lashing. There was no time to worry about that now. She needed to act quickly before whoever these people were sent for reinforcements to search the warehouse.

Julia eased out of her hiding place and looked up and down the narrow pathway. She stood still, closed her eyes, and listened to the sounds of the building. She thought she could still hear the progress of the man with the gun. The sun was at an angle that illuminated an aisle two rows over. It was wider than the others and she thought it might lead her to the reception area. There was a pathway once removed from this main aisle and, keeping close to the stacks of containers, made her way toward what she thought to be the front of the building.

Cautiously Julia peeked around the stack of crates stamped with a crown encircled with a garland of flowers. She could see the door to the reception area. No sound reached her ears. This was her chance. She sprinted from the safety of the shadowy protection of the crates and grasped the doorknob. It was locked. Her heart sank with dismay as a heavily accented voice just behind her said, "Going somewhere?"

It was the man with the gun. Julia felt the blood leave her head and for a moment she felt a little faint. Before she could respond, another man stepped from the shadows to the right of the door and said, "Hello, Julia."

Julia jerked around at the sound of Viktor Letov's voice. She was speechless.

"Has the cat got your tongue?" he asked.

Julia cleared her throat. "Hello, Doug."

He smiled, that same wolfish smile she remembered from their first date. "Come, come, Julia. Surely Mitch has told you my story by now."

She remained silent.

"Why are you here?"

"I'm looking for Renee Slovaska."

His looked pensive for a moment. "Very well. Come and meet her."

With that he linked her arm through his and turned her back into the bowels of the building.

The woman sitting behind the desk in the bumped-out office at the rear of the building looked up from the paper shredder she was feeding. She rose to her feet. "What are you doing? Why is she here?"

Viktor gestured for Julia to have a seat. She remained standing. The man with the gun stood behind her. He shoved her into the chair. Viktor cast an annoyed look in the man's direction then focused his attention on Renee Slovaska.

"This is Ms. Julia Hampton of the Hampton Detective Agency." He smiled down at Julia. "She wanted to meet you."

"I know who she is," Renee Slovaska snarled. "I just don't know why she's here, in my office."

She turned off the paper shredder. "This complicates everything. Now we will have to deal with her."

"Since she was snooping around the warehouse, we were going to have to deal with her anyway," Viktor said.

Renee snatched a stapler from the desk and threw it forcefully against the opposite wall. "Imbecile! It's one thing to suspect, and quite another to prove. You've played right into their hands."

"We've moved way past suspicion, dearest step-sister, and now we not only have Marisha broadcasting all she knows, but now this one."

"Another idiotic mistake. When are you going to start thinking with your head!"

Julia glanced at the man with the gun in the hope he was distracted by the bickering between Viktor and Renee. No such luck. He stared back at her, a knowing look in his eyes, as if he dared her to try to run. She lowered her gaze and saw, just beside the wastebasket in the corner of the room, the curl of a long gray tail. She quickly averted her eyes.

Renee picked up her cell phone and read a text. "The car will be here in a couple of minutes. Take care of this mess and meet me at the rendezvous." She withdrew her purse from a bottom drawer of the desk. "If you're late we're taking off without you."

Julia listened to the sound of Renee's retreating footsteps with a growing sense of dread. The room became very quiet. She glanced up to see Viktor studying her. He smiled when he caught her eye. "Don't worry, doll. No one's going to hurt you."

"But Vik—" the man with the gun started to argue.

Viktor held up his hand in a gesture for silence. "Ms. Hampton is the daughter of a very wealthy man, Grunt." He folded his arms across his chest and swayed back on his heels. "Let me emphasize *wealthy*. Not rich, not loaded, but wealthy. Do you understand the difference?" He shrugged. "Never mind. The point is, what do you think will happen if any harm comes to the only child of a very wealthy and powerful man?"

The gunman shifted from foot to foot. "Renee said—"

"I know what Renee said. She's upset. She hasn't thought this thing through." He paused for a long moment. "The Feds need me and so far, that's worked in our favor. I even think, with a little cooling off, they'll come to appreciate me again."

The gunman remained silent.

"I like to keep my options open. So, here's what we're going to do." He grinned at Julia. "Let's give Ms. Hampton a nice quiet place to contemplate the cost of sticking her nose where it doesn't belong."

"Not here in the warehouse."

"No. This is too easy. If she found it, they'll be on to it soon."

"So where?"

Viktor ignored the question. He held out his arm to Julia. When she drew back from him, his left eyebrow shot up and he shook his head. "This could be a lot uglier than it has to be, Julia. Do yourself a favor and come along like a good girl."

Julia felt a sense of reprieve that Letov didn't see any advantage in killing her. She hesitated then took his arm. It was pointless to resist, she reasoned. She could either go to her confinement in one piece or she could go there lame and incapacitated. Those were her choices for there was no hope of escaping two violent criminals armed with a rapid repeat gun. She chose to rely on her wits and a sound body.

Viktor looked over his shoulder at the gunman and nodded. The rapid firing of the gun into the computer tower made Julia jump and squeak in fear. Viktor patted her hand where her grip had tightened on his arm. "Just a little housekeeping, Julia. Nothing to be alarmed about."

The leisurely attitude Viktor had displayed up to this moment changed. He propelled her quickly through the building and out a door into a back lane behind a row of buildings identical to the one that housed the Fine Art and Antiques Shipping Company. The gunman followed close on their heels.

Julia couldn't stop herself from glancing back. She caught a glimpse of Callahan as he tracked behind them. The gunman turned to see what had caught her eye and fired a single shot at Callahan.

Julia gave another little squeak and Letov swore as he quickened their pace to almost a run.

"Idiot! It's just a damn cat!"

They rounded the building on the end of the row and there stood a line of empty cargo containers.

Letov opened the second in the line and shoved Julia inside. He brushed his hair back with both hands and straightened his jacket. "It'll be cool again tonight, but I think you'll be safe enough from the elements in here." He started to turn away from her then grinned. "Go ahead and bang and yell all you want. It's the weekend." The grin turned into laughter. "You won't disturb a soul." With that, he slammed the door closed and drove the lock home.

Julia sank to her knees and started trembling. She was safe, after a fashion. Now that the imminent danger of the last twenty minutes was over, she gave in to a debilitating lethargy. She sat there until the quaking inside began to ease off. When she could focus her mind, she began to assess her situation.

The gunman had shot at Callahan. Julia didn't know if he had hit his mark or not because Letov had jerked her along the path. Dax would be heartbroken—and she would as well—if the Grunt's aim had been true.

She glanced around the dim interior of the container. It was old, rusted in spots, and not air tight. She could see pinpoints of light where the hinges of the doors attached to the structure and along the seams of a vent high in the wall at the front of the oblong structure. She got to her feet. It was time to get herself out of this mess.

* * *

Mitch had gone another round with the lovely Marisha, she of the orangey red lipstick and tight spandex. The only revelation there was that she was terrified to return to Tampa.

He closed his eyes and rubbed the bridge of his nose. He had had little sleep since Julia Hampton entered his life and Woodrow Hampton's words were becoming a self-fulfilling prophecy. Peter Ryder was missing, Trip Youngblood had been murdered, Viktor Letov had vanished, and now, Viktor's compatriot, known fondly in criminal circles as the Grunt, had also slipped his surveillance.

The Marshals Service did not look like the highly trained, proficient law enforcement body it was touted to be.

He couldn't worry about that at the moment. The tarnish on the Service's star was the least of his concerns. He opened his eyes and took the file folder from his desk. It was time to see what Debbie Williams, claim secretary of the Weatherby Insurance Agency, knew about all this business.

She was an attractive woman, Mitch thought as he entered the interview room. A little older than what Viktor usually gravitated toward for his many trysts, but still an angle worth exploring. Viktor liked the ladies and the ladies, at least for a while, liked Viktor. According to Sandra, the receptionist, it had been their joint idea, hers and Debbie's, to post Viktor's profile on the dating site, Couples Connection.

"Sorry to drag you down here so early, Ms. Williams." Mitch pulled out the chair across from her and sat down. "Did anyone offer you coffee or something else to drink?"

"I'm floating in coffee, Deputy. I was hustled out of

bed and brought down here only to sit and wait for hours. What's going on?"

Mitch opened the file and picked up a photo of Viktor Letov. "You know who this is?"

She glanced down at the photo. "Of course. That's Doug Heinz. We work together."

"How long have you known him?"

She gave her head a small shake and shrugged. "I don't know, nine, ten months. Less than a year."

"How did you meet him?"

"At work." She frowned. "Look, what's this about? I was due at the office an hour ago. No one here will even let me call to tell them where I am." She was working herself up to righteous indignation. "They took my cell phone." She hesitated. "Can they do that? Just take my cell phone?"

"A man was killed last night." Mitch paused for affect. "Murdered."

The woman paled. "Doug is dead!"

Mitch pulled another photograph from the file. It was a head shot of Trip Youngblood as he lay on the slab at the morgue. "How about this man? Do you know him?"

"No," she shook her head, paused, "yes. Maybe."

Mitch let the silence build as Debbie Williams took the photograph in her hands and looked at it more closely. "He's dead, isn't he?"

"Yes."

"I do know him, but I don't know his name." Two parallel lines formed on her brow as she concentrated. "I've seen him with Mr. Weatherby, at the office. He may be a client of the agency, I don't know, but he was in and out of the office several times a couple of months ago."

She wouldn't look at Mitch as she passed the photograph

back to him. He took his time replacing it in the folder.

Debbie rested her hands on the table then lowered them to her lap. Her gaze traveled from the table top to the closed door then the mirror on the wall, never once coming to rest on Mitch.

Finally, he broke the silence. "You work in the claims department at the Weatherby Insurance Agency, correct?"

She nodded and looked down at her clasped hands.

"Does Doug Heinz work claims?"

Debbie cleared her throat. "No. He brokers coverage for high profile policies."

"High profile?"

She shrugged. "Malpractice coverage for physicians, yachts, special events, expensive items not routinely covered by our normal policies."

"Art, you mean? Jewelry?"

She nodded.

"Art exhibitions?"

She glanced up at him, paled, and looked quickly away.

Bingo, Mitch thought.

"Okay, Ms. Williams. We appreciate your patience and your help." He stood and closed the file. "You can collect your phone from the front desk."

Debbie Williams was out of her seat and out the door almost before he could settle back into his chair. Mitch sat, his arm resting across the closed file, and stared at the doorknob. After a moment he roused himself and left the room.

He retrieved his gun from his desk drawer. Jones came through the back door of the office as he was securing it in his shoulder harness. "Did they put a trace on Debbie Williams' phone?"

Jones nodded.

"Any contact with Viktor since yesterday?"

"Yesterday morning was the last time he called her. She texted him just before noon to say she needed to talk to him. No response. Nothing today."

"Put a tail on her. Get two men and another car with us. Chappie has had all the beauty sleep he's going to get."

Jones eyed Mitch, frowned, then nodded. "Right." He took out his cell phone and placed a call.

* * *

The two extra deputies were deployed to the rear of Chappie's house as Mitch and Jones approached the front door. Mitch rang the bell and they heard the faint echo of the chimes. He waited a second before he pounded on the door. There wasn't a sound to be heard from the interior. He pounded again and was at the point of kicking it in when he heard the deadbolt turn. Both men had their guns at the ready when the door opened.

"What's the meaning of this?" Chappie demanded as he stood there in his pajamas, his dressing gown hanging open, and a pair of silk slippers on his feet. His hair was tousled and a clear adhesive strip covered a line of tiny stitches on his left cheek. At the sight of the drawn guns, he started and took a step backwards, almost tripping over the dangling sash of his robe.

"Good God!" he said as he regained his composure. "What in heaven's name is going on?"

Mitch stepped past Chappie and did a quick scan of the foyer and stairwell. He nodded at Jones who went from room to room on the ground floor of the house. Chappie's face flushed with indignation.

"I demand an explanation." He jerked his arm free of Mitch's grasp as he propelled him into the morning parlor. "Have you gone mad?" He gathered the sash of his dressing gown and tied it around his waist.

Mitch returned his gun to the holster and motioned for Chappie to take a seat. Chappie stood his ground and puffed out his chest. "Where is Adoni? Why are you here at this ungodly hour, making enough noise to wake the dead?"

"Adoni?"

"The butler."

"Right." Mitch rubbed his forehead, sighed, and motioned once more for Chappie to have a seat.

This time Chappie complied; his bravado having vanished in the aftermath of the moment. He cleared his throat. "What's this about, Deputy Lawson?"

"Trip Youngblood."

"Trip?" Chappie adjusted the lapels of his dressing gown. "Good Lord, man. Couldn't you have waited for a more civilized hour to question me about Trip?"

"It's almost nine-thirty, Mr. Chapman."

"My point exactly. Besides, why would you want to talk to me about Trip? He wasn't the injured party last night. I should think you'd be here on my behalf."

"Well," Mitch said as he sat in the armchair facing Chappie, "that's why I'm here. Who do you think would want to kill you?"

"Kill me!" Chappie reared back in his chair and clasped a hand to his chest. "But last night you said you didn't know who the target was."

"True, but the bullet did graze you. If everyone hadn't

drawn back when the cat attacked Heinz, the bullet might have found its mark."

"You think Trip was the target?"

"Why would someone target Mr. Youngblood?"

"They wouldn't. I mean, to my knowledge, there's no reason why anyone would want him dead."

Chappie settled more comfortably against the back of his chair, ready for a good gossip. "Unless you know something I don't, Deputy."

Mitch looked out the long floor-to-ceiling window at the artful flower garden on the side of Chappie's house. He stood, walked over to the window, and looked down the side lawn to the two-car covered parking at the rear. "You have a car, Mr. Chapman?"

"Of course. Two, in fact."

"A Jaguar and what else?

"A Land Rover."

"Where's the Land Rover?"

Chappie rose from his chair and came to stand beside Mitch. "Well, it isn't in its parking space so I imagine Adoni went out in it."

"The butler?"

"Butler, assistant, general factotum."

"How did he come to work for you?"

"If you must know," Chappie turned from the window and sat in the armchair again. "I hired him while I was in Milan. Three years ago."

"He's Italian?"

"Georgian, actually."

"As in Russian Georgia?"

"As in Russian Georgia."

"Is there a last name for this Adoni?"

"Bunin." Chappie frowned. "Is this really any of your concern, Deputy? Shouldn't you be out checking fingerprints or doing bullet tests, checking out the usual suspects?"

"It's rarely the usual suspects, Mr. Chapman. What did you do after you left The Club last night?"

"You know good and well what I did. I went to the hospital. My plastic surgeon came, stitched up my face." He touched his bandaged cheek gingerly. "And I came home, had a stiff brandy, took a sedative, and went to bed."

"What time did you leave the hospital?"

"Oh, I don't know. It took forever for Stevens to get there. He was at a dinner party and didn't want to rush off and leave the hostess hanging. Can you believe that? Said the medical staff didn't think my injury life threatening."

"So, what time would that be?"

"Oh, one o'clock, I think. Maybe a few minutes after." He stood, crossed the room to the door, and pulled a long, braided cord, seemed to remember that Adoni wasn't there to answer his summons and swore. "God, what I'd do for a cup of tea."

"Trip Youngblood is dead."

Chappie's jaw dropped. "Trip! Dead!" He returned to his chair, fell into it, and ran the fingers of one hand through his hair. "He was the target? Why would anyone want to kill Trip?"

"Good question."

Chapter Seventeen

I wouldn't have figured The Grunt for a good shot, especially on the run as he is, but I feel the burn across my left hind quarter. Perhaps his low brow denotes only lack of intelligence, for I consider myself quite agile and capable of outmaneuvering the ordinary common criminal.

The Voice and his muscle have rounded the last building in the row with Julia firmly in their grasp and are now out of sight. Darn pain is nothing to sneeze at. I do believe that panting sound is me. That won't do. I've got to keep up. Julia's life depends on it. But first I'll take a little breather, just for a moment, and take stock of my wound.

It appears to be nothing more than a flesh wound but my sleek coat is a bloody mess. I can take it. I have to keep going and find Julia.

The dead end that confronts me as I round the last building is desolate. Nothing stirs. There's no sign of either Julia or the thugs who took her. I put my nose to the cracked and pot-holed street and catch her scent. She's here, in one of these large containers.

"Yeow!"

"Callahan!" She bangs on the inside wall of the metal, sending percussive shock waves through my sensitive ears. I hear the sound of receding footsteps from within then running feet and a loud thud against the closed and locked opening. Julia moans.

I check all around the door and make my way along the exterior of her prison. There are a few rusted spots at ground level, but they are too small to allow even a mouse to enter. From what I can determine, there's no way out except through the container door. A long metal rod forms the locking mechanism. This is one of those times when I would give anything for opposable thumbs and height.

There's nothing I can do to free her except go for help. I can only hope she doesn't injure herself badly by continuing to throw her body against the locked door. I call out to her one last time and head to the water's edge. From here I get my bearings. The landmark bridge is up river to my left. I know where I am, and I turn right and follow the waterfront.

* * *

Mitch found Jones on his cell phone, leaning against the car when he left Chappie's house. He stood when Mitch approached, placed the phone in his inside jacket pocket, and cleared his throat.

"You need to call Gerty."

"Gerty?"

Jones held up his hands in that I'm-just-the-messenger expression and slid into the passenger seat of the car.

Mitch pressed the speed dial for Gerty. Standing in front of the car, he listened, then flipped the phone closed and slammed his fist against the hood. "That darn cat."

He put the blue light on the roof for the short sprint from Chappie's to the vet clinic. Gerty stood by the front door waiting for him. "Three deputies?" Jerking the door open to the clinic, he sent the bell suspended from it into a spasm of jangles. Gerty followed on his heels, her mouth shut, her expression grim. "One civilian managed to evade all three of you." Mitch shook his head as a young woman with freckles across her nose scurried from behind a counter and opened the door separating the waiting room from the interior of the clinic. She looked as pale as Gerty and she eyed Mitch with apprehension.

Halfway down the hallway a man in a white lab coat with ginger hair stood in front of an open door. When Mitch was a few steps from him, he gestured into the office. "Deputy Lawson."

"What happened?"

The veterinarian closed the door and turned to face him. "She brought in a cat that she said needed medical attention."

"I know that much." Mitch tried to modulate the hostility in his voice. "How did that become an escape from a security detail?"

The vet indicated a chair across from his desk but Mitch ignored the offer. The vet remained standing as well. "Perhaps because I didn't know she had a security detail. My question is why would she have one?"

Mitch was in no mood to share. "For the reason the word implies."

The vet was beginning to get an attitude of his own.

His shoulders went back and his brows arched. "Because of her father's paranoia or something more specific?"

"Do you really think three deputies of the U.S. Marshals Service would be combing the alley behind your office if this was a case of paranoia?"

The vet frowned. "No, I suppose not." He sighed. "Look, she called and said she thought her cat had a cold or something. I have office hours on Saturday until one o'clock, so I told her to bring him in."

He shrugged. "When she got here, she said that it was a false alarm, that the cat was fine."

"Did you check the cat?"

The vet blushed. "Well, no. She didn't seem to think it necessary."

"And that didn't seem suspect to you?"

"I'm a veterinarian, Deputy Lawson. Julia is a friend of many years. She isn't a pet owner, never has been to my knowledge. I just assumed she was overly apprehensive about her friend's cat and then thought better of her worries."

"You didn't think it was unusual for her to leave through the back door?"

"Well, yes, a little. But she said she was avoiding someone in the waiting room. I assumed it was just someone she knew, that she had a busy day and didn't want to get caught up in a long-winded conversation with one of my cat ladies."

"Right." Mitch stared at the stack of files atop a file cabinet to the right of where the vet stood. He never should have left her safety to someone else. "Damn it." His focus returned to the vet. "Did she say anything else? Anything that might indicate where she was headed?"

"No." The vet's cheeks turned a rosier pink. "She mentioned the Juan Diego Florez performance next month."

Mitch watched the color deepen in the young man's face and he swore to himself. *Our little Julia was a master at distraction.* Well, he wouldn't be so easily manipulated, not again. When he got his hands on her, he was going to ring her lovely neck.

He went out the back door, looked up and down the alley, and scanned the buildings. He spotted three security cameras. Maybe they would get lucky, but in the meantime, where to start?

Mitch turned to Gerty who had been shadowing his every move. "What about her cell phone?"

Gerty shook her head. "She left it at the apartment."

"What did she do all morning?"

"Paperwork. She sat on the sofa with some files and her laptop." Gerty's face was red with shame. "She made a couple of calls. I heard her ask for a Horchow. The second call was to someone called Chappie but I got the impression she didn't speak to him."

"Anything unusual happen? Anything that would have set her off on a wild goose chase?"

"No." Gerty glanced away then looked him in the eyes. "I took coffee to the deputies on guard."

"Uh huh."

"And her father came by. He was upset about the Youngblood murder."

Mitch felt his stomach drop. "Did he know she had been on the scene?"

"I don't think so. He was upset but not *that* upset." Gerty shifted from foot to foot. "He seemed okay with the trip to the vet. I think he thought it might keep her out of the investigation."

Mitch nodded. "You're probably right. I'm sure he knows all of Ms. Hampton's little tricks." He glanced down at Gerty and gave her a pat on the upper arm. "We'll find her."

The gesture didn't seem to alleviate Gerty's sense of responsibility. She merely nodded. "I'll start with the owners of these buildings for their security footage."

Mitch walked to the end of the alley. When he got to Bull Street, he looked up and down. Which direction would she have taken? There was no way to know. The only clue they had was Julia's activities of the morning.

The vet clinic was only ten minutes from Julia's house. He saw the deputy still at his post when he drew up to the curb. The look on his face was wary as Mitch walked past him and up the steps.

He strolled through the apartment, taking in everything. The clothing pushed to the floor from the bed the previous evening, the disarray in the closet, a cold cup of coffee on the end table by the sofa. There was a half-eaten Danish on a delicate china plate on the kitchen island. A matching small plate, clean of any evidence of food, sat on the floor by the pantry door. The darn cat, he thought.

He took out his phone and called Jones. "Bring Chapman to me." He closed it and sat on the sofa where Julia had spent the morning and opened her laptop. After several attempts, he gave up on the password and turned his attention to the files on the coffee table. Something in these files had convinced her to risk her safety by ditching her security team. He had to find what it was. By all rights, he should call her father and let him know the situation, but he couldn't bring himself to do that just yet. His motives for this delay were a muddle of pride, remorse, and a need he couldn't identify.

All that aside, if Julia didn't turn up soon, her family would have to be informed.

* * *

Julia sat on the floor of the grimy shipping container and rubbed her left shoulder. She now knew two things. Callahan was alive though on his own in an unknown environment, and the door to her prison was solid and locked.

The container was warm, the sunny fall day having heated the metal. She knew that warmth would fade quickly as the sun began to set. She didn't relish the thought of spending the night trapped there.

She got to her feet. It was useless to worry about Callahan. All she could do was hope he stayed close until she could find a way out of her current predicament.

Her hair fell to her shoulders as she pulled the long curving clip from the French twist. She tested the strength of it and decided it would do if she were careful not to apply too much pressure.

Julia assessed the potential weak spots in the construction of the container. The vent, while the most rusted and potentially fragile, was too high overhead and too small. Her only hope was the door.

All the hinges were rusted to varying degrees. The container was old and probably hadn't been used in many years, but because of its age it was built of sturdier stuff than newer, lighter containers.

She poked and pried at all four hinges of the double doors and settled on the lower left corner. It appeared to be the weakest. If she could pry it away from wall, then perhaps she could kick at that corner of the door and create enough space to crawl free.

Well, that's the plan, she thought, as she settled on the floor, flexed her fingers, and began picking at the bubbles of rust with her hair clip.

She kept at it steadily until her fingers cramped so much she had to take a break. The flesh of her fingers was red and there were places where the continued prying motion and rust debris had broken the skin. She shook her hands and took a few laps around the container to stimulate the flow of blood to her lower legs.

It felt good to move around. She tried to ignore the burning in her hands by letting her thoughts drift to Callahan and how he might be faring. There had been no further indication of his presence since that initial crying out. Dax was going to be very unhappy with this turn of events, that was certain. Her father would be paralyzed with worry. She stopped in her tracks. Until now she hadn't given any thought as to how her disappearance would affect her mother and father. Especially her father.

Mitch would have learned what she had done hours ago. Was it hours? She looked up along the roofline of the container at the pinpoints of light seeping through the rust holes. The light was still bright. She had been at the vet office shortly after nine. Could it be only noon? She didn't know. It was seldom that she wore a watch anymore and she had purposely left her phone at home for fear Mitch's team would track her through it. The inability to see outside left her uncertain as to how much time had lapsed. All her conspiring to evade her security detail now came back to haunt her. No one knew where she was, and she had no way to monitor the passage of time or to reach out for help. If only she hadn't been so vain.

Julia slumped down with her back against the wall of the container. There it was, the truth of the matter. In her vanity, her desire to prove her ability to solve this case, she had managed to get herself into an impossible situation and to cause those who loved her to suffer. Why had she needed to win so badly, to be the one with the answers? Why wasn't it enough that she knew she was capable, that she could take care of herself? She sighed, flexed her fingers and returned to the door.

"Okay," she said. She closed her eyes and took a deep breath. Slowly she let it out and opened her eyes. She ignored the pain in her hands and took up the hair clip. It was chipped down to less than a third its length. Soon it would be useless.

* * *

I keep to the south side of the street as I make my way along the river. It lies in shadow due to the slant of the sun and affords me some camouflage. Two concerned pedestrians have tried to lure me into their care since I hit the more touristy area of River Street.

One of the riverboats is docked, tourists are lined up to board for the trip down to the fort and back. A child spies me and makes a beeline in my direction. I take evasive action and reach the tunnel under Factors Walk. It's cool inside the cobbled arch way, and I slip behind a newspaper dispenser and catch my breath. The pain in my hind quarters is now a constant throb but not unbearable. I don't understand this sudden need to rest, but rest I must. After a few minutes I'm panting less. Time to move on. The sun has passed its crest and I still have many blocks to travel to reach Julia's house.

The stone steps up to Bay Street are a struggle but I reach the top and size up the traffic.

Normally I would take the nearer route straight across, but I know my strength has been sapped by my injury and therefore, my speed. This isn't a time to play dodge with tons of motorized metal. I walk to the crossing and sit and wait for the pedestrian light to turn green.

A car comes to a stop at the traffic light. A woman lowers her window, puts her head out, and calls to me. "Here, kitty, kitty. Are you hurt?"

I can't allow myself to be sidetracked by the concern of strangers. I hurry across Bay Street, past the Holiday Inn and down Bryan Street. If I can only keep up this pace, I'll soon reach Calhoun Square. There's bound to be law enforcement hanging around.

Chapter Eighteen

Mitch closed the file and returned it to the coffee table. He was no closer to a clue as to Julia's whereabouts than he had been at the beginning of his search. His team was checking with Uber and city cabs but so far nothing had turned up.

She had the cat with her and that helped to a degree. Callahan's presence would limit the range of possibilities.

Her car was in its usual parking space in the garage. A call to the manager of The Cloister had given them nothing. The shipping company that had handled the two Russian losses was located in Miami. The owners of the Fechin were in Cozumel for a family wedding and not due to return for another week. Tallulah Youngblood was supposedly in Milan, Italy. Mitch had agents trying to determine if that was the case or not. It didn't help when you were dealing with people with the means for flying on private jets.

Chappie sat on the sofa in Julia's living room, his legs crossed at the knees, and an ebony cane with a gold knob leaning against it. He looked the picture of health except for the small clear bandage on his left cheek and not at all put out by having been summoned to another interview.

Mitch remembered Rocco Sullivan's comments on Chappie's penchant to gossip. He moved to the windows overlooking the street and said, "Tell me about Rocco Sullivan."

"Which version?"

"How many versions are there?"

"Well," Chappie settled more comfortably into the cushions of the sofa, "there's the factual stuff. You know, his profession, friends, involvement in the community." He smiled. "Then there's the innuendo, the half-truths, the back-of-the-hand whispers." He arched an eyebrow at Mitch. "I imagine you're interested in the latter."

"So tell me." Mitch settled in a chair across from Chappie. "Let's start with the back-of-the-hand whispers."

From his expression, Mitch knew Chappie found this avenue to his liking. "Well, he came to Savannah some thirty-five to forty years ago. Set up his little antique shop and, I suppose, managed to make a living. Then about thirty years ago he began to deal in art, not just the occasional interesting piece that came his way through an estate or lucky find at a yard sale. He was suddenly dealing in serious art. He caught the fancy of Aloyis Mercer and she pretty much made him. People began to believe his claims that he was an expert."

"And you doubt his competence?"

"I wouldn't say that, exactly. I mean, anyone can educate themselves to a certain level of proficiency in any given field and I suppose all those years of grubbing around in dusty attics did help refine his eye for detail."

"But he wouldn't be your choice of authority if you were planning a major art purchase?"

"Something like that."

"Do you know about the stolen Fechin?"

"Savannah is a small town, Deputy. Besides, it was all over the news when it happened."

Mitch glanced at his watch then studied Chappie. "And Adoni. What does he know about art?"

Chappie sighed. "Well, he *is* art, isn't he? A living, breathing, walking piece of art."

"You met him in Milan?"

"Yes."

Mitch looked over Chappie's shoulders and out the windows at the trees in Calhoun Square. "Did Tallulah Youngblood also know Adoni in Milan?"

Chappie looked surprised. "How did you know?"

"Just a hunch. When was the last time you saw Tallulah."

"Tuesday. She popped in briefly for coffee."

"At your house?"

"Yes. Actually, Adoni picked her up at The Cloister. She was in town on business about her grandfather's estate."

"Is she on good terms with Adoni?"

"Adoni doesn't discriminate, Deputy."

"Good to know." Mitch stood in the middle of the room, lost in thought, then glanced at Chappie. "Handel will take you home."

Chappie stood and picked up his cane. At the doorway

he turned back toward Mitch. "Trip was my friend, you know. I want you to find the bastard who did this."

It seemed that in that moment the elegant façade slipped. For an instant Mitch saw before him an aging little man, rather ridiculous in this day and age with his pinstriped suit and vest, the bowtie a shocking pink, the gold tipped cane, the sparkle in his eye extinguished. It only lasted for a second and then Chappie was himself again as he gave a mock salute with his cane and went out the door.

Mitch glanced at his watch. He would have to tell Julia's parents that she was missing. It was past time. He moved to the window and watched as Chappie was settled into the waiting sedan. Just as he was about to turn from the view, a movement caught his eye. It was a gray cat, limping along the sidewalk in the shadow of the bushes along the perimeter of the square. "Callahan!"

He bolted down the stairs and out the door. He scooped the cat up and felt the sticky wetness on his fur.

"Yeow."

The ground seemed to shift under Mitch's feet. The cat was hurt. He had approached the house from the north along Abercorn. Julia had to be somewhere in that direction.

He cradled the cat in his left arm and dug his phone out of his pocket. "Set up a grid north to the river. Block by block foot search. Check every door, alley, garden." He trotted toward his car. "She may be hurt." He closed his eyes and swore. "And bring her father and mother to the apartment."

The vet was just leaving the clinic when Mitch drew up, lights flashing, siren wailing. The receptionist had already locked the door. He pounded on it and she appeared on the other side, her eyes round as saucers in alarm. One glance at the cat in Mitch's arms and she unlocked the door.

"What's this?" The vet stood in the doorway separating the waiting area from the rest of the clinic.

"He's hurt." Mitch gently placed the cat in the vet's arms. "There's blood along his back legs."

They went through to an examination room. The vet eased Callahan onto the table and pulled on a pair of latex gloves. He probed Callahan's hind quarters and the cat swiped at him with a forepaw and cried out.

"It's a long straight line of broken skin along his left flank. Very symmetrical." He took a bottle of clear liquid and doused a large cotton gauze. Gently he swabbed at the injury until it was clean of blood and debris from the streets of Savannah. "I'd say he slid down something extremely sharp. The muscle is cut but not all the way through. It's not the least jagged so it would have been quick, before he had time to react and create a tearing pattern."

"What could cause a wound like that?"

The vet shook his head. "I couldn't say. I've never seen an animal injury quite this smooth and clean."

Mitch folded his arms, ignoring the blood on his jacket. "A gunshot?"

"Gunshot?" The vet stared up at him. "Here in the city? Surely not."

"Will he be okay?"

The vet had been probing Callahan's lower legs and underbelly. "Nothing else seems to be affected. I'll stitch this up and we can keep him calm for a few days. It should heal nicely."

The cat was the only clue to Julia's whereabouts. Mitch wasn't about to leave him at the vet's office. "Bandage him up. I'll wait."

"You should leave him here. He needs to be crated so he doesn't further injure himself."

"I'll take care of him."

"I don't know. Julia…"

"Julia will expect the cat to be at home when she returns."

"Returns from where?"

"Good question."

* * *

Mitch knew Woodrow and Audrey Hampton were already at Julia's apartment when he returned with Callahan in tow. As he mounted the steps, a vintage Rolls Royce pulled up, stopped in the middle of the street, and a chauffeur equally as vintage got out of the driver's seat and proceeded around the rear of the vehicle at a slow, stately pace. He opened the rear passenger door and handed Ethel Hampton out onto the sidewalk. Mitch came forward and offered his free arm.

Aunt Ethel looked smaller, if possible, and ashen, but her spine was straight and her eyes blazed.

"Well, young man, what have you got to say for yourself?"

"Nothing. It's all my fault."

"I'm afraid Woodrow will agree with you." She patted him on the arm. "But I know how hard it is to ride herd on the Mercer women."

"Mercer?"

"My mother was a Mercer." She looked up at Mitch. "You didn't know."

He shook his head. He should have known. It was his job to know things like that. It explained a lot, why her father was so protective, why, for all her bravado, there was a shadow of self-doubt beneath Julia's assured, lighthearted façade. Not only were the Mercers known for their wealth and philanthropic activities, but for the fatal kidnapping of Christian Mercer nearly forty years ago.

Audrey Hampton sat on the sofa, back erect, legs crossed at the ankle, her hands folded in her lap.

She looked up when Mitch and Aunt Ethel appeared in the doorway. Her husband was pacing the floor, hands clasped behind his back. He stopped and stared at Mitch as if he were an alien being.

Mitch handed Callahan off to Aunt Ethel and stepped forward. "Mr. Hampton—"

Woodrow Hampton caught Mitch unprepared with a right hook that made him stagger. Gerty started forward and Mitch held up his hand to stop her. For a moment he thought Julia's father would strike him again but instead Woodrow turned his back and crossed the room to stand, staring out the window.

Audrey Hampton rose to her feet. "Well, now that you've got that out of your system, Woodrow, perhaps we can find out what happened and what's being done to find Julia."

"Every man we have, as well as local cops and the FBI, are combing the city." Mitch refrained from rubbing his jaw. "We know Julia left Dr. Claiborne's office at nine-forty."

"You let her go to the vet on her own?" Woodrow Hampton faced him now, murder in his eyes.

"No. She had a detail, but your daughter is clever, Mr.

Hampton. And persuasive."

Aunt Ethel moved to the armchair and collapsed into it with Callahan still in her grasp. "You know it's true, Woodrow. When Julia makes up her mind to do something it's impossible to stop her."

He wasn't ready to be dissuaded from his anger. "And the crime scene? You let her go to Trip's house, to see his dead body?" He ran his hand through his hair. "What kind of law officer are you?"

"Stop it!" Audrey Hampton took a deep breath. "What's being done and what else can be done? What kind of resources do you need?"

"We feel she's north of here, somewhere between here and the river." He glanced at the cat. "It's the direction the cat came from."

"What does the cat have to do with it?" Woodrow turned his glare on Callahan.

"He was with Julia when she lost her detail."

Audrey crouched by the sofa and held out her hand to Callahan. "He's injured." She glanced up at Mitch, her already fair complexion paler than death. "You don't think…"

Callahan sniffed Audrey's fingers then hopped onto the coffee table. Woodrow sneezed. The cat sat on top of the files and looked up at Mitch. He blinked slowly three times.

Woodrow sneezed again. "What *do* you think, Lawson?"

Callahan adjusted his position and a paw snaked out and pushed the files to the floor.

"I think the cat wants to tell us something." Mitch bent over and scooped up the papers that had fallen from the top folder. The top sheet was a bill of lading from The

Fine Art and Antiques Shipping Company. The address read Miami, but the receiving stamp showed a date and a partial address in Savannah.

"Boss." A young female officer poked her head around the doorway to the kitchen. "We've cracked it. The password to her laptop."

"What was it?" Mitch asked as he and Woodrow crowded into the kitchen on the heels of the computer tech.

"Russian for Fechin fan."

It would be funny if it wasn't so serious. "Her browser history. Now."

The tech moved the mouse and clicked on the computer's history. They scanned the last half dozen web addresses. She had looked at the auction house in charge of the Youngblood estate, the gallery that sold the Fechin to the Peltiers, and twice at the Fine Art and Antiques Shipping Company. Mitch clicked on the last link for the shipping company and saw the dockside address and a convenient Google map.

"How in the hell didn't we know they had an office in Savannah?" He glared at the tech, then Gerty before he turned and headed out the door and down the stairs. He was on the phone as he went.

"Cordon the whole docks area this side of the Talmadge bridge. All the manpower we have. Go in silent."

Chapter Nineteen

I almost made it. Aunt Ethel is quick for a woman her age. If my injuries hadn't slowed me down, I'd be with The Lawman right now. They'll never find her without my help. I limp to the window. It's closed and locked. How am I going to get out of here?

Gentle hands scoop me up from my perch.

"Come on you. Keep an old woman company." *She holds me close and whispers.* "I'm frightened for the child."

I can feel a mild tremor in the hands that lovingly caress my back. I begin to purr and nestle my face against her neck. It is all I can do for Julia at the moment.

* * *

Julia sat with her back against the side of the shipping container. Her hands were torn and raw from digging away at the metal around the hinge of the door. She held them between her knees and pressed, hoping to distract herself from the pain. The nub of a hair clip lay at her feet. She had kicked and kicked against the unyielding corner of the door. The only reward for her effort was a slender separation from the wall of the container. If she pressed her face against the door, she could see a sliver of the building opposite her with her right eye.

The view allowed her to judge the time. Shadows from the stacks of containers reached halfway to the roof of the building opposite her. She closed her eyes and pictured the waterfront in the fall.

The sun rode low in the southern sky at this time of year. The positioning of the containers was toward the river, to the northeast. Early afternoon, then. That wasn't so bad. As she'd labored away at the rusty hinge, she had imagined the day almost at an end. Still plenty of time, she thought. Someone would find her. Mitch would find her.

She rested her head against the side of her prison. Her arms trembled with fatigue. Her throat was parched. She felt lethargic with the warmth of the container. Her eyes closed and her mind drifted, lighting on one random thought after the other; Aunt Ethel with Callahan in her arms, Mitch smiling down at her, Debbie with her head buried in a file with Doug…"

Her eyes flew open. What was it about that scene? The file folder that disappeared the moment Doug blocked her view of the desk. What did she know about Debbie?

Julia struggled to her feet and began to pace the container. She needed to move, to dispel the lethargy. There was something in that behavior, she knew it in her bones.

She only knew Debbie through Sandra. When had she

started working for the Weatherby Insurance Agency? Julia tried to force the memory. An older woman with steel gray hair had been the claims secretary at one time. When had Sandra first mentioned Debbie? Julia couldn't remember.

Okay, she told herself. Focus on Viktor. His photo had been familiar to her because she had seen him at the agency at some point in time over the summer. He hadn't piqued her interest enough then for her to even remember having seen him.

Let it go, she told herself. Let it go and it'll come back to you. Another approach then. Viktor was the agent on the two art thefts but not the estate jewelry. But the watch Viktor wore was from the Youngblood estate, Julia was sure of it. She couldn't get past the doubt that Viktor had stolen the art. It was too easy to connect to him. The jewelry, on the other hand… Who would think an agent with the company was involved?

"There are two thieves." Julia stopped in her tracks. She was suddenly convinced this was the case. Viktor had thought he could regain his standing with the FBI in spite of stealing the jewelry. If he had killed Trip Youngblood, he would know there was no going back. "And I would be dead." She shivered at the thought.

Julia went to the door of the container, laid flat on her back on the grimy floor and began kicking with both feet at the loosened corner. Trip had been murdered for the Russian painting, not because he had blown Viktor Letov's cover. Peter Ryder was missing and Julia feared he was dead. Who was behind it? She had to get out of the container. Other lives might be at risk.

* * *

The Fine Art and Antiques Shipping Company warehouse was surrounded by plain clothed officers. The entire six blocks on either side of the area was locked down tight. Mitch and Jones took the lead. The door was unlocked. They rounded the opening, guns drawn. No one was in the reception area. They listened to the sounds of the building for a minute then repeated the procedure into the warehouse proper.

Additional officers filtered into the building behind them. They quickly and efficiently searched the structure. It only took them minutes to locate the office and the shattered computer.

Mitch stared at the bullet holes and felt a moment of panic.

"No blood." Jones pulled on a pair of latex gloves as he glanced in Mitch's direction. "I doubt there's anything salvageable on the computer but I'll check everything else."

"Right." Mitch said. "Right." He took a deep breath and began to reconstruct the scene in his mind. The computer had obviously been destroyed to hide any trail back to whomever was running this operation. A jumble of iron pipes was sprawled all over the pathway twenty-five feet from the office.

This was probably what set off the spray of gunfire into the computer. Julia, he thought, spying on Viktor and his cronies.

They had her, there was no doubt in his mind. Would he kill her? Mitch couldn't let that possibility take root. Viktor had the criminal mind of a reptile. He would be out for his own best interest. Julia was a commodity, a very valuable commodity. Viktor had known about Julia's pedigree all along. The clue had been there in Viktor's computer search of The Bank of Savannah. That was why he had ingratiated himself, wormed his way into her life when the opportunity presented itself.

Always out for the main chance, that was Viktor Letov.

So, what would he do next? That was the million-dollar question. Blackmail was the most obvious answer. Prior to turning evidence against his cronies Viktor could have easily pulled off such a stunt.

Did he think he could get away with it on his own? It didn't matter. Mitch was going to find him. And Julia.

He turned his mind to the more immediate problem. There was no blood here so where had the cat been shot? That would be the trail to Julia.

A back door opened onto an alleyway behind a long line of buildings. The most likely exit, Mitch thought, if you had just fired off a rapid repeating gun into a computer tower. Gerty was already in the alley, sweeping side to side in search of clues. Mitch joined her and they each took a side.

Fifteen feet along he saw the spot of blood. He looked back along the concrete until he found the divot where the bullet nicked it. Just beyond that he found where the bullet ricocheted into the side of the building.

Gerty called out to him. She was about forty feet away and she stood over the shell casing. "He fired from right about here. One shot."

One shot. Mitch repeated it in his mind like a mantra. Only one shot. They continued their search to the dead end, following a trail of blood droplets. A long line of old storage containers stacked against the back of more buildings ran to the right. The blood trail led them straight to the second container in the row. It looked as if the cat spent a bit of time here, possibly resting from his injury, before heading off to an opening between the containers.

Mitch followed the blood trail a few feet further but kept glancing back at the second container.

Suddenly the sound of pounding against metal rang through the alleyway and Mitch and Gerty rushed to the door. The latching mechanism gave easily enough, and the door swung open. There lay Julia, on her back, grimy from head to toe, her feet raised in preparation for slamming the door again.

He had her in his arms before he could stop himself. He held her close, kissing her forehead, her cheek, then her mouth. His knees were weak with relief. For a long moment he just held her, pressing her face against his chest, allowing his heartbeat to slow down, for his world to stop rocking.

She was alive. She was safe and he was never going to let her out of his sight again.

Then he was angry. So angry that he could have punched through the metal of the shipping container with his bare fist. "Julia!" He disentangled her from his embrace and shook her. "What in the hell got into your head? You could have been killed!"

Tears stood in her eyes and began to roll down her cheek. "Oh, Mitch." Her lip trembled. "I was so afraid."

The image before him tore at his heart. His beautiful Julia with her hair all awry, full of debris from the container, face smudged, her clothing stained and soiled. Then he saw her hands. He lifted them for closer inspection. "What in the hell happened?"

She sighed and leaned into his body. "Gold isn't the strongest material. The next time I'm trapped in a metal container, I'm going to put my hair up with a good, solid, iron hair clip."

The humor was her armor, Mitch realized. She was trying to compose herself, to combat the lingering fear, so he answered in kind. "But it won't be nearly as charming."

She smiled then, and he wiped the tear tracks from her face. "Come on," he swooped her up in his arms, "your father has already punched me in the jaw. I'm afraid he'll take a bull whip to me if I don't get you home soon."

Her arms went around his neck. "Oh, Mitch. I'm sorry."

"I'm not." He grinned down at her. "Now I have an excuse for you to kiss away the pain."

She smiled then placed a gentle row of kisses along his jaw line. "Better?"

"You think you're getting off that easily?"

Julia laughed and he held her tighter, took a calming breath, and headed for the alleyway. Gerty had removed herself to the corner of the dead end when they opened the container door and she saw the way the wind blew. When Mitch came abreast of her, he saw she couldn't quite hide her grin as she called in the result of their search to the command center. He couldn't help but grin, himself.

* * *

The shock and stress of the day and previous night had taken its toll on Julia by the time Mitch got her home and her mother got her into the bath. She didn't even have the energy to be annoyed that her father had armed security in the foyer, the stairwell, the living room, and probably on the roof.

She sat docile as a lamb as Aunt Ethel dotted ointment on her hands and gently wrapped them in gauze. Aunt Ethel had been a godsend, persuading her father and mother to go home and leave Julia to rest. It was a short-lived victory, Julia knew. The thing that had persuaded them was her promise to return to Ardsley Park before the sun set. But for now, she needed the comfort and quiet of her own home.

Callahan looked up at her as she approached the bed. The white bandage around his hind quarters in stark contrast to his gray fur. "Poor kitty. Can you forgive me?" She crawled between the sheets next to him and scratched his ears. The sound of his purring grew louder and Julia found that comforting.

She was so tired. Aunt Ethel gently rocking in the chair under the window and Callahan purring at her side had the desired effect. Julia felt on the edge of sleep. She was home, in the cocoon of her comfortable, safe world. A little niggle at the back of her mind tugged at her. She needed to see Mitch.

There was something he should know. But the lethargy took over and she drifted down into deep, restorative sleep.

Chapter Twenty

Mitch nodded at the private security guard as he entered Julia's apartment. Aunt Ethel was just coming out of the bedroom with a tray in her hands. Mitch took it from her and carried it to the kitchen. He returned to the living room to find Aunt Ethel standing at the window, staring out onto the square.

She turned to him and smiled. "She'll be all right. We're a tough lot, despite the outward trappings."

He nodded. "Can I see her?"

"She's asleep."

"And how are you holding up?"

She chuckled. "Haven't you heard? I'm a tough old bird. Nothing much gets to me."

"That's not true."

She turned from him and when she spoke her voice sounded huskier than usual. "I've lived a long and full life. There aren't many stones I've left unturned." When she faced him again, the twinkle was back in her eyes. "I've quite enjoyed scandalizing the Mercer Hamptons."

He laughed.

"I've always thought Julia had a bit more of me and my mother in her, but the shadow of Christian Mercer has made her afraid to be herself. He was my brother's grandchild." She took a seat in the armchair. "I blame Woodrow but of course he can't help himself. He was very close to Christian. They grew up as close as brothers." She blinked at the tears forming in her eyes. "Christian was only eleven. Woodrow a few months younger." She sighed. "Well, enough of that. Tell me about the man who did this."

"We have him." Mitch watched as Callahan sauntered in from the bedroom, went to Aunt Ethel's chair, and waited for her to pick him up. "The Feds caught him and his sidekick at a small airstrip just out of town. It was already under surveillance because it's known to be used by drug traffickers." He walked over to the chair where Aunt Ethel sat with the cat on her lap and scratched behind Callahan's ears. "I just dropped by on my way to interrogate him."

"I want to go with you."

Mitch and Aunt Ethel turned at the sound of Julia's voice, to see her standing in the doorway to the bedroom. He walked over to her and took her hands in his, turning them over to examine the bandages. It was difficult for him to look at her face, to see the softness of sleep on her features, the gently mussed hair.

Aunt Ethel cleared her throat. "I need a cup of tea." She unceremoniously dumped Callahan to the floor and made her way to the kitchen.

"How are you?" he asked as he let his fingers trail up Julia's neck to her face and into her hair.

She pressed her cheek against his palm, closed her eyes, then opened them again slowly. "I'm fine. Really." She rose to her tiptoes and kissed his jaw. "The question is, how are you?"

"I'll never live that down, will I?"

She smiled a slow, lazy smile. "Never."

He wanted more than anything to stay but he knew he couldn't. Viktor Letov sat cooling his heels in a cell at the courthouse and Mitch needed to get a crack at him. The Feds were happy they had their key witness safely under their control again. It had taken the implied influence of Woodrow Hampton to get them to grant him a few minutes with his chief suspect in the murder of Trip Youngblood and possibly Peter Ryder.

He sighed. "I have to go."

"Take me with you."

Mitch shook his head. "No, Julia. Not this time."

She started to protest then something in her eyes changed. "Okay."

"I want your word you'll stay put."

"I promise."

"I'll be back to take you to your parents' house later."

She nodded.

He turned for the door and she caught at his sleeve. "Mitch. I don't think it's Doug—Viktor." She ran her hand through her hair. "Not all of it anyway."

He waited.

"It doesn't fit. He's a lifelong criminal. Until now he's been smart, ahead of the authorities all the way. He took the jewelry, yes. I don't doubt that. The Youngbloods have been Mr. Weatherby's clients for decades. He made the changes to the coverage for the estate after Nils Youngblood died, as a matter of formality. He's ninety-two years old. He'd never make the connection. Viktor knew that. So why would he risk stealing from his own clients? Why leave a trail right to his door?"

"I agree. And that's what I'm going to find out. That's why I need to know where you are at all times, Julia. I can't worry about your safety and do my job." He slid his hands up and down her arms as if to warm her. "Understood?"

She nodded. "It's about the history, you know. It has been all along. Someone is fascinated with the Romanovs, the grandeur of their reign, that moment in history. Someone with a lot of power and money."

"Yes. And this town is the mother lode of money and history." He gave her a swift kiss and went out the door.

* * *

Julia sat staring out the window, her mind a thousand miles away. Aunt Ethel came into the room bearing a tray with two cups of tea.

"Here you go. This will make you feel better."

"Why do we always think tea will make things better?" Julia took one of the cups and sipped it.

"It's familiar. It gives off heat, just like the cat. That's reassuring, comforting. The process as much as anything takes us out of the moment. Grounds us."

Ethel settled into the comfort of the sofa and the cat crawled into her lap. They sat in silence for a while then she said, "He grounds you, doesn't he?"

"Yes."

"Then I guess he's the one."

"Yes, he's the one."

They were quiet again, each woman looking back across the span of their lives.

"He reminds me of Gus Haus and the summer of 1946. He was the strong, silent type, too. Knew when and how to take charge." Aunt Ethel chuckled. "I love a man who knows how to take charge."

"Aunt Ethel!" Julia laughed. "You're worse than Granny Mame."

"Life is for living, child. You only get one go round. Don't let the sorrows of others dictate what your life will be." She shooed the cat out of her lap and struggled up out of the feather pillows of the sofa. "I'm going home. Regis will be here with the car soon. You pack a suitcase and go home to your parents. They need comforting."

"I know." Julia stood and kissed her aunt on the cheek. "I'm sorry I caused everyone such worry. I know it was headstrong and selfish."

"Well," Aunt Ethel patted her cheek, "I know how it is to live in a fishbowl. My father stayed in a panic about what I'd do next. I have regrets about the worry I caused him and my mother, but I don't regret my life." She retrieved her handbag from the bombe chest in the foyer. "A little prudence is wise but don't live in fear."

"I think I've always been afraid and just didn't know it." Julia leaned against the archway of the foyer. "I'm not afraid anymore."

"Good." As Aunt Ethel went through the apartment door she called back to Julia. "Don't feed the cat. He's finished off all the dim sum that the militia didn't eat for lunch."

Julia returned to the sofa and took Callahan into her lap. "You're going to be so fat Dax will have to put you on a diet."

Callahan closed his eyes to golden slits and turned his face away from her in a look of contempt.

"Right. As if anyone could tell you what to do." She scratched his ears and under his chin until he forgave her. "You'll have to keep to my rooms when we go to Ardsley Park. Daddy is allergic, you know."

Callahan flattened his ears, sighed then went to sleep on her lap.

* * *

Viktor Letov looked very sure of himself as he smiled across the table at Mitch. He knew the Feds prized him over a conviction for robbery and that their needs would take precedent over any local infractions of the law. The only leverage Mitch had was a murder charge. He didn't believe Viktor had killed Trip Youngblood, but he hoped the threat could be used to prompt the gangster into revealing something useful.

"So, Viktor, where were you going?"

"A little vacation."

"Your former associates getting too close?"

"Maybe it wasn't me they were shooting at, but, hey," he shrugged, "you can't be too careful."

"A lot of people are looking at you for a lot of reasons."

"So?"

That grin again. Mitch wanted to smash his face. "So, murder takes precedent over information. Even the Feds have to concede to that."

"The girl's okay. Maybe a little pissed but I didn't lay a

hand on her."

"I'm not talking about the girl. I'm talking about the owner of the watch." He upended the manila envelope that had been lying on the table and out slid the Rolex.

"Okay, maybe I shouldn't have used the story old Weatherby told me about the watch, but you know what they say. A little truth always makes a lie more believable." He sighed and sat back in the chair. "Yeah, I stole the watch and a few other trinkets. So what?"

"So, after Trip Youngblood caught you out, he ended up dead."

Viktor didn't respond immediately. Mitch could almost see his lizard brain working.

"That was nothing to do with me. Looks like the shooter wasn't after me. I'd say he found his target after all."

"But you'd be wrong because in the sweep for you, we also scooped up Anna Kuzmicha." It was Mitch's turn to smile. "An old friend of yours, I believe."

Viktor had no response.

"Tell me about Debbie Williams."

"What about her? She works at the insurance agency."

"I get the impression she's more than a fellow employee."

"There's no reason you should." He shrugged. "I took her to dinner a couple of times. Just fitting in, you know? That's what you wanted me to do, wasn't it? Besides, she's a little past her prime, if you know what I mean."

"Maybe she told one of her Russian friends where you were."

"She doesn't have Russian friends."

"You sure about that?" Mitch opened the file in front of him. "Adoni Bunin. What do you know about him?"

"Nothing. Never heard of him."

Mitch studied Viktor for a long moment. As much as he hated to admit it, he believed him.

"Tell me about the Fechin. How did you come to be the agent?"

"Mr. Weatherby got a call from the owners about insuring it. Weatherby doesn't do much anymore, so he turned them over to me. I wrote the policy. My half-sister works for the shipping company. I might have suggested they use her company for the transport. There's no crime in that. It just fell in my lap and that's what I'm supposed to do, right? Marking time till I can testify and split?" He lifted his hands in a dismissive gesture. "It disappeared and by the time the museum wanted coverage on the clothing, the news coverage of the theft had begun to die down, so I wrote that policy, too. The old man is just a figurehead at the agency these days. I don't know how he's still kicking."

"These things just fell in your lap, and you decided, what the heck, and filched them."

"No. I'm not stupid. Especially after the painting went missing. There was a lot of heat and I didn't want my name near any of it." He sat forward, his forearms resting on the table. "Jewelry, that's easy to turn over. Art, that's more complicated and takes time. And the clothing? Who would want it?" He shook his head. "No, man, it wasn't me."

Mitch collected the watch and the file. "We'll talk again."

Viktor smiled. "No, Mitchell, we won't. I'm heading for L.A. Enough of these backwater little places. I'm going where there's some action. And you won't be going with me. Or haven't you heard? I'm getting a whole new security team."

* * *

Mitch stood on Chappie's porch, listening to the faint chimes resounding in the house. After a few minutes Chappie came to the door. He still wore the suit and vest he had on earlier in the day, minus the coat. A pair of reading glasses rested on the end of his nose.

"Deputy Lawson." His eyebrows shot up. "Three times in one day. I'm beginning to think I should have the spare bedroom made up for you." He gestured for Mitch to enter, and he closed the door.

"What now?"

"Debbie Williams."

"Oh, that creature!" Chappie waved his hand as if swatting a fly. "Totally useless. I don't know why Weatherby has her in claims. She doesn't know anything about anything." He started off down the hallway and motioned for Mitch to follow. "I'm just in the study trying to make heads or tails out of the jumble in here. Adoni usually takes care of things and I need the number for the moving crew." He sighed and took a seat behind a desk. "You can't have just any Jake leg off the street to handle museum quality pieces."

"You reported the theft to Miss Williams?"

"Well, I called Weatherby first. You can imagine my reaction when the staff opened an empty crate." He moved some papers around on the desk, his eyes darting from one thing to another. "But the old man told me to call the claims department." Chappie scowled. "A quarter of a million dollar policy and I'm just supposed to call the claims department."

"What happened when you called?"

"Nothing." He threw the scraps of paper in his hand onto the desktop. "The damn woman took my name and phone number and that was all. I had to call back the next day. I got lucky and Peter Ryder was in the office. He didn't even know about the theft."

Mitch moved to the window overlooking the formal garden at the rear of the house and, at the bottom of the lawn, a garage apartment over the open parking bays. The hunter green Jaguar didn't appear to have moved. The space next to it still stood empty.

"Where's your butler?"

"Damned if I know. But you can bet I'll find out when he returns." He fell against the high back of his chair and sighed. "I'm useless with all this," he gestured at the files and odd circulars and papers on the desk. He placed two fingers of his right hand against the artery in his left wrist and sat quietly for several seconds. He released his wrist. "See what it's done to my blood pressure?"

"Does your butler know Miss Williams?"

"I don't know. Maybe." He paused for a moment. "He probably spoke to her about the claim. This has been a real problem since we discovered the loss two weeks ago and, honestly, that's what I have him for, to deal with the little difficulties in life."

"When was the last time you discussed the claim with anyone?"

"Tuesday, I think. Ryder came to the house. Wanted me to describe blow by blow what I saw when the crate was opened. How the packaging looked, had it been tampered with," he waved his hand, "as if I would know."

"Does the museum still have the crate?"

"I don't know. The police looked over everything,

wrote a report, took a ton of photographs, and told me to call the insurance company. Ryder asked the same thing when I first talked to him on the phone. I suppose he could have it."

Mitch turned from the view out the window and realized Chappie was watching him.

"Would you like a drink, Deputy? You look like you could use one."

"Thanks, but I'll pass." He crossed the room to the study doorway. "If the butler shows up, ask him to call me."

"It's not a matter of if, Deputy, it's a matter of when. Adoni does have his appetites."

"Good to know." He turned to leave. "I'll see myself out."

Chapter Twenty-One

Julia studied the legal pad on her lap. She was curled up on the sofa, Callahan warming her feet, and the detritus of the three insurance claims strewn all around her. The pad contained several lists. She had spent the time since Aunt Ethel left trying to arrange the facts to prod her subconscious. It was a trick she learned during her decorating career. Put something in and take something away. After a while, the remaining pieces fit to create a beautiful picture.

Today the exercise wasn't working. She flipped to a new page and stared at the empty lines. What was the common denominator in all the cases? At the top of the page, she wrote: the Weatherby Insurance Agency. All the stolen objects were insured by the same company. What else? Two insurance policies had been written by Viktor Letov and one by Mr. Weatherby. Not enough consistency there but she drew a line dividing the page. In one column, she listed the Fechin and the clothing. In the other, she listed the jewelry heist.

What else? Peter Ryder had worked the initial phase of all three claims. She added his name to the list with an arrow directly to the agency.

She stared at the diagram and after a few minutes she put an X through the jewelry heist. That issue had been resolved; she was sure of it. Retrieving the stolen items might prove to be a problem but the *who* of that mystery had been resolved to her satisfaction.

After a while she realized nothing else was going to filter through her weary brain. She tossed the pad onto the coffee table and began to randomly pick up pages from the various files. She noticed Youngblood's signature page on the old original policy, a notarized certificate of authenticity on a document relating to the Fechin portrait, and a pink message slip from Reginald Horchow's original claim. None of it sparked that intuitive fire that usually led her in the direction her mind needed to go.

Julia sighed, laid her head on the pile of cushions stacked against the sofa arm and closed her eyes.

The sound of the door softly closing caused her to open her eyes. Mitch came strolling into the room with that walk that sent her heart racing. She heard the door open and close again. The security guard stepping out to allow them some privacy, she decided.

He came to sit on the edge of the sofa where she lay. "Alone at last."

She smiled. "How on earth did you manage that?"

"I have friends in high places." He grinned. "And I carry a gun."

"What now?"

"I would like," he sighed, "to kiss you just once without an audience."

"Be still, my heart. I don't know if I could stand it."

"It's powerful stuff, I admit. But I think you're up to it."

He was right. It was powerful stuff. He's the one, she thought, as Mitch proceeded to show her what an old-fashioned necking session was all about. But she would have to take it slow. She knew instinctively he wasn't the settling kind of man.

They broke apart and she laid her cheek against his chest, listening to the beat of his heart. "If I didn't know better, I'd think you missed me."

"Only collecting my just rewards." He moved his lower jaw side to side. "You owe me."

"How long are you going to play that card?"

"Are you trying to negotiate out of it already?"

"I don't know. I might need persuading that there's something in this for me."

"It's an onerous chore, I admit, but a man's gotta do what a man's gotta do."

He was about to kiss her again when Callahan decided he'd had enough of these shenanigans. He hopped onto the coffee table and said, "Yeow!"

Mitch scooped him up and cradled him in his arm. "You're always putting a spanner in the works." He scratched behind Callahan's ears and stood. "Darn cat." It was said with affection but the interruption served to bring both Julia and Mitch back to earth.

"Your parents expect me to have you safely home before dark."

Julia rose from the sofa, tugged gently at Callahan's scarred right ear, and went toward the bedroom. "I won't be but a few minutes."

She changed out of her sweatpants and tee shirt. Her overnight bag was already packed. With a quick brush through her hair and a dash of lipstick she was ready to go.

When she returned to the living room, Mitch was looking through the yellow legal pad at her scribblings.

"Trying to make the pieces fit together," she said, "but no luck so far." She gathered up the files and notes and stuffed them into her briefcase. She handed the overnight bag and briefcase to Mitch and lifted Callahan from the coffee table. "Ready."

* * *

The early evening traffic was light and it took them no time to arrive at the 45th Street home of Julia's parents. Mitch helped her out of the passenger seat of the car as he scanned the Tudor mansion in the heart of the Chatom Crescent neighborhood. Directly across the street was Guckenheimer Park.

"Nice digs."

Julia blushed. "It's home."

"Uh huh."

A butler opened the door when they were a few feet from it. He could easily blend in with the Secret Service detail for the President, Mitch thought. He noted the earpiece wire trailing down into the collar of his shirt.

Her parents, they were informed, were out by the pool

having drinks. Mitch followed Julia through the house, taking in the subtle details of wealth. He let his gaze travel over the artwork, softly lit by an unseen source, silver that gleamed in the low light of lamps, rugs that were faded and worn.

Nothing over the top, almost homey in the sunroom.

Julia handed Callahan off to a maid who had a crystal bowl filled with what looked like pate waiting for him on a placemat on the floor by the door to the pantry. He offered up no objection.

The pool looked deep enough to get a good workout. The layout of furnishings around it invited you to sit and relax. He noted the wrought iron fence, the three-car garage, a carriage house overlooking the area. A glimpse of movement told him the second story of the carriage house was a lookout point for security. It was positioned to give a good view over the street beyond as well as the entire outdoor space at the rear of the house.

Mrs. Hampton offered Mitch a drink, but he declined. He could tell from the look on Woodrow Hampton's face that he was still in the doghouse. That was fine by him. He didn't feel he could breathe in this setting.

"Stay for dinner, Mitch." Julia's eyes pleaded for him to accept the invitation although her voice revealed nothing more than the courtesy that it was.

"Another time," he said as his cell phone vibrated in his pocket. He took it out and read the text. "I have to get going anyway. Duty calls."

"What?"

"Nothing but paperwork." He said good night to the Hamptons.

Julia walked him to the front door. "What?"

He shrugged. "Nothing to worry about. They're shipping Viktor off tonight and if I want another crack at him, I need to get back."

"Do you think there's anything more he can tell you?"

"He's observant, always out for the main chance, so he might have seen something that would be helpful." He took her hands carefully in his and rubbed his thumbs along the backs of them. "I won't know unless I try."

"Okay. But you'll call me if there's anything new?"

"Sure."

"And Mitch…"

"Yes?"

She started to speak but changed her mind with a little shake of her head. As she turned to close the door, she called after him, "I'm going home tomorrow morning. I'd like it to be with you."

"Good to know."

Mitch stopped with his hand on the door handle of the car and gave Julia's home a good look. It was impressive in a low-key kind of way. But then, that's how the truly wealthy lived, he decided. He bet none of the Hamptons even knew what Ramen noodles were, much less that they'd ever eaten them.

He got into the black service sedan and took out his phone. The message was from Gerty. *We have a floater.*

Mitch turned the key in the ignition and set out for Fort Pulaski, his headlights probing the early dusk.

Tourists roaming around Cockspur Island in search of a picnic spot in the late afternoon had discovered the body trapped in the rocks used to beef up the shoreline.

Flood lights and the white privacy tent marked the spot. They were lucky. If it had gotten beyond Goat Point it would have been lost to the ocean. It wasn't a pretty sight.

Most of the back of the skull was missing. The ME was wrapping up his initial examination of the corpse when Mitch arrived.

"How long has he been in the water do you think?"

"Three or four days, at least. Maybe more."

"Any ID?"

"We should be so lucky. I'll try for prints when I get him back to the lab. Can't promise any results. The body's too far gone. And it's Saturday."

Mitch noted the medical examiner's golfing attire and grunted. "It's the life."

"Ain't it just."

Gerty was waiting for him by his car when he hiked up from the riverside. She had her laptop resting on the hood of his car.

"I think it's Ryder," she said. "The height is good; he has the gray hair and a beer gut."

"Did Ryder have a beer gut?"

"Probably," Gerty said. "Old guy, living alone, giant screen TV, and not much else. I'd say most likely." She pulled up a photo of Ryder but it was only a head shot. "Can't tell much from the extremities, too much bloat. Doubt we'll be able to get prints."

"You're probably right about that."

The body had been loaded into the van. The harbor police had begun to dismantle the crime scene paraphernalia. They knew they wouldn't learn much from the location. Whoever it was had floated from somewhere upstream along the Savannah River. Mitch stood and looked east to the sea. Nothing but empty darkness. To the west a rosy glow hugged the skyline of Savannah. Another day in the books.

Gerty had been waiting patiently beside him. He

glanced at her. "Call it a day, Gerty. It's been a hard one."

She closed the laptop. "It's the job."

Mitch grunted. "What the latest on Letov?"

"Gone. And good riddance, I'd say."

"Yeah. He's not our murderer. At least not these murders." He felt weary to his bones. "What about the Land Rover?"

"Nada."

It had indeed been a long, hard day and Mitch couldn't remember when he'd last slept. He thought of Julia safely at home in her ivory tower then turned his mind from the memory. Best not to go there tonight when he was weary and frustrated. Tomorrow was another day.

He got into the sedan and turned the car in the direction of the sparse, small garage apartment he called home.

Chapter Twenty-Two

Tired as she was, Julia didn't enjoy a restful night's sleep. It had nothing to do with the murder of Trip Youngblood or the theft of Russian artifacts. It was the look in Mitch's eyes as he helped her from the car and surveyed the irrefutable evidence of her life.

Living as she did in an apartment upstairs from her office had lulled her into thinking she could be someone other than Julia Mercer Hampton. Though he had known who she was, the full impact of what that meant hadn't been real to Mitch until he stood before the family pile.

The morning was ebbing away and just when she decided he wasn't coming to collect her, Gerty arrived at her door. Julia found this more telling than any looks or polite excuses.

She took a deep breath, smiled at Gerty, and invited her in.

"I'll wait by the car."

Gerty's comment was no less telling than if it had been Mitch saying the words. The message was clear. This was not the world of a deputy. Julia refused to let her feelings show in her expression or her voice. "Okay. I'm ready. Just let me grab Callahan."

They drove in silence after the initial how did you sleep, are the hands feeling better, have you had breakfast, conversational gambits. When they pulled up before her door, Julia turned to Gerty.

"I'm going to run upstairs and leave Callahan. I won't be a minute."

"Where are you planning to go?"

"To the Telfair Museum. I need to check some things."

Gerty shook her head. "No, no, no. Mitch said to bring you home and sit—not to leave your side. That's what we're doing."

"If that's what you're doing, then it'll have to be at the Telfair Museum because that's where I'm going." Julia hopped out of the car and ran up the steps to her front door with Callahan struggling in her arms. The door opened as she reached it and she nodded at the security guard who closed it firmly behind her.

Callahan wriggled free of her embrace the moment she entered the apartment. He tried to make a break for it back onto the stairwell landing, but she caught him in the nick of time.

"Forget that, mister. You are supposed to stay calm and quiet and heal. No more climbing out windows, sneaking up on the mafia, or general mayhem. You're staying put."

Julia put water in a bowl for the cat, grabbed a charger for her cell phone, and slipped through the apartment door and down the stairs. She could see Gerty on her phone through the sidelights of the front door. By the time she reached the car the phone was nowhere in sight.

"I'm sorry, Gerty. You don't have to do this. I have plenty of security to trail around after me. I'm probably safer than the President."

Gerty shook her head in a defeated manner, started the car, and pulled out into traffic.

The museum was only a few blocks away, but the tourist traffic of a Sunday morning had the streets clogged with tour buses and day trippers. When they arrived at the museum Mitch was there, leaning against the hood of his car, his arms crossed, his expression unreadable.

"Why are you here?" Julia asked.

"Because you're here."

"Believe it or not, Deputy Lawson, I managed quite nicely before you came into my life."

"Believe it or not, Miss Hampton, that was then. This is now."

Julia threw up her hands in exasperation. "What's that supposed to mean?"

"Now that I know how adept you are at getting yourself into life threatening scrapes, I can't, in good conscience, leave you without a minder."

"Of all the…" She saw the light in his eyes and shook her head. "Really? Is that all you can come up with? Lamest excuse I ever heard," she teased.

"It's the best I could do on such short notice."

Julia felt the heaviness on her heart lift. They were back on solid ground, or close to it. The reserve of the previous evening was less pronounced. "Well, since you're here…"

Mitch's phone rang and he held up a finger as he took the call. "Lawson." He listened. "On my way."

He pushed away from the car and opened the door. "You need to go home with Gerty. The museum can wait."

"What's going on?" She caught his arm. "Mitch, you said you wouldn't keep me in the dark. I need to know."

"A body was found late yesterday." He motioned for Gerty who had kept a discreet distance to give them privacy. "I have to attend the autopsy and learn what I can."

"Mitch!"

He hesitated, sighed, and said, "Let Gerty take you to my office. You can wait for me there. You can't go off on your own anymore, not until we find the link."

Julia took a calming breath. "Is it Ryder?"

"I can't say. I'll know more after the autopsy."

"Okay." She stepped back from the car as he slid into the driver's seat. "I'll see if I can find anything we might have missed in the files. But, Mitch," she placed her hand on top of the rolled down window, "I won't wait forever."

"Deal." With that, he shifted the car into gear and tore off down the street.

When they got to the courthouse, Julia retrieved her briefcase from the back seat of the car and followed Gerty up the back stairs to the Marshals' offices. Julia was deposited at Mitch's desk and Gerty moved off to her own corner of the large open room that served all the field agents. Once Gerty stored and locked away her gun, she glanced across at Julia with an *eyes on you so no funny stuff* expression then turned her attention to her computer screen.

Julia sat back in Mitch's chair and surveyed the items

on his desk as she swiveled the chair back and forth. This was his world, what made him tick. It held the ordinary implements of an office worker: phone, computer, stapler, notepad, pen, and one of those hand-held springy things you used to build strength in your hands and arms by squeezing it. Nothing on the desk suggested who it belonged to.

She stole a glimpse in Gerty's direction then opened the desk drawers one after another. The first one was where he kept his gun. It was lined with a soft felt cloth. A partition midway in the drawer separated the space into a second compartment with ammunition and nothing else. The lock was substantial.

In the next drawer, she found a pile of small spiral-bound notebooks. She took a couple of them out and flipped through them. Case notes, she realized, in an abbreviated code probably only known to Mitch. The only identifying information was the occasional date or a name. One of them was simply a list of times going on page after page.

There wasn't much of interest in the other drawers until she came to the bottom one. Inside she found envelopes addressed by hand to Mitch, many with foreign return addresses. At the bottom of the drawer was a photograph of a man in full dress military uniform. It was the image of Mitch but the age and sepia tones of it suggested otherwise. She studied it until a clerk came walking through the row of desks with papers in her hand. Julia slipped the photograph back in place and closed the drawer.

Two other deputies worked at their desks, as did Gerty. Otherwise, the room was quiet. Julia glanced around to ensure no one was paying her any particular attention and she booted up Mitch's computer. There was probably a long list of regulations prohibiting a civilian from accessing the Marshals' network but she couldn't resist the opportunity to see what their evidence was.

The computer was password protected. Julia sat back in the chair and thought a minute then she opened the middle drawer of the desk and rooted around in the clutter of paper clips, extra staples, pens, pencils, and rubber bands until she found a computer tech's card. She turned it over, typed in the numbers and letters written on the back, and watched as Mitch's computer screen came to life. Men, she thought.

What she saw as it booted up was an image of herself standing on the sidewalk, a glimpse of Viktor Letov's damaged car barely visible in the foreground.

It was what she saw in her expression in the photo that stilled her fingers from moving past the image. She stared straight into the camera, her lips slightly parted, one hand capturing a wisp of hair back from her face. It was as if she'd been caught in a moment of revelation. Perhaps awareness was a better word. She wondered what Mitch saw when he looked at it.

She shook off the feeling of being exposed and began to scroll through the photographs. There were quite a few of them, starting with the damaged car, her house from different angles, numerous shots of Viktor Letov at different locations. Toward the end of the file were shots of the warehouse on the docks, the shipping container where she had been imprisoned, and the last one, a photo of the yellow legal pad sheet she had been doodling on the previous day.

"Huh." What about her doodling had been interesting

enough for Mitch to photograph it? She lifted her briefcase onto the desk and took out all the files on the three cases. After staring at the page for several minutes, Julia realized there was no message there to discern. Half the equation had been resolved with the arrest of Viktor Letov. How much of the Youngblood jewelry would be recovered remained to be seen. She scratched through the left side of the diagram, marking out the jewelry. Then she drew a line through Peter Ryder's name. There wasn't any doubt in her mind that the body in the morgue would prove to be Peter.

What she was left with was the Weatherby Insurance Agency. She turned to a fresh page and listed the agency on one side at the top. Beneath that she started adding anything and anyone associated with the agency. Mr. Weatherby didn't seem like a suspect for murder, but she included him anyway. Also on the list were Sandra, Debbie, Viktor, Chappie, Mr. and Mrs. Peltier, Reginald Horchow and Tallulah Youngblood. Fechin, King Christian IX, Valentin Serov, Rolex, and jewelry comprised a sub list.

On the opposite side of the page, she made the heading Russian / Russian Art. Beneath this she listed Fechin, King Christian IX, and Valentine Serov. She was making a sub list of people with a connection to this category, starting with Viktor Letov, when Mitch strolled into the office, stopped beside her, and read over her shoulder.

"What thing is not like the other?"

"Something like that." She threw the pen onto the pad and sat back in the chair. "Was it Ryder?"

Mitch nodded. "Dental records proved our worst fears."

"Two people dead. That is so awful. And all for art."

"Art may be the ultimate goal, but greed is the catalyst.

We just need to find who would most benefit financially from the sale of these items."

"How are we going to do that?"

"Let's start with your list." He gestured toward his desk chair and she stood and stepped aside.

Mitch moved the mouse and the computer screen sprang to life. He looked up at her. "Naughty girl."

"I was bored. Besides, leaving your password on the back of the tech's business card in plain sight isn't the most secure way to protect your computer."

"In plain sight?"

"Pretty much."

"Uh huh."

Julia pulled the visitor chair around and sat beside Mitch as he instigated a search of the people on her list. All kinds of institutions began popping up from banks to the IRS. "You can do that? Don't you have to prove cause or something?"

"This is just preliminary stuff. You'd be surprised what records you can access if you know the right key strokes." He opened a separate screen while those searches were running and showed her a list of files already reviewed by his staff since the beginning of the investigation. It was an impressive list from phone records and social media to property holdings.

On the face of it, Chappie and the Peltiers looked like the financially sound and upstanding citizens they claimed to be. Reginald Horchow's file was slim but it didn't suggest anything suspicious.

Tallulah Youngblood had more money than God. If Mitch's hypothesis was correct, then none of these people were suspect from a financial viewpoint. But could they be involved because of the other side of the coin; art for its own sake.

Mitch sat back in his chair and studied Julia's list. "Letov is the only Russian listed."

"He's the only Russian involved, to my knowledge, unless you count his step-sister, Renee Slovaska."

"You listed Trip Youngblood."

"His Russian painting was stolen. The Peltiers are listed for the same reason."

"Why isn't Tallulah Youngblood on the list?"

"I wasn't finished, but I don't think she fits. I'm not sure who in the family will inherit Trip's estate but if she wanted it, she could have worked out the possession of the Serov with the family."

Julia let her gaze run down the list. "Besides, it wasn't a real quality piece. Tallullah has a bit of her grandmother in her. She only wants the best."

"Who's her grandmother?"

"Aloyis Mercer Youngblood."

"You're an incestuous lot around here, aren't you?"

"Well, she really isn't a Mercer. She married one but there were no kids from that marriage. She also married a Higgs and finally a Youngblood."

"Earned her money the old-fashioned way, did she?"

"No. Higgs was the first husband. She married him for love, they say, and he married her for her money. The others were all about sleeping with the company you plan to keep and producing an heir."

"Uh huh."

Julia could have bitten her tongue off. What made her say such a thing? There were times when Aunt Ethel just popped out of her mouth. She was glad Mitch continued to stare at the list because she could feel the heat in her face. There was no way to retrench from her faux paus so she decided the only way out was forward. "Tallulah and her brother are the children of Aloyis' only child."

"And which Youngblood would that be?"

"Satch. Trip's uncle."

"Satch? What kind of name is that?"

"Satchell is a name from Aloyis' side of the family."

"Of course it is. I suppose there was money there as well."

"Tons."

"So now Tallulah has it all?"

"No. As Trip said, there are Youngbloods all over Georgia and along the east coast. But Satch and Aloyis were at the top of the heap of their generation as far as money went. I imagine most of Trip's wealth will go to Tallulah and her brother but there'll probably be some smaller bequests to other members of the extended family. Trip never married."

"How do you keep all this stuff in your head?"

Julia shrugged. "The port of Savannah may be the fourth largest container seaport in the U.S. but the city itself is a small town at heart, regardless of the population. At its core are people who have known each other for generations. It doesn't seem complicated to me, but I suppose it's something of a tangle for others."

"I guess you'll have to be my genealogy source for this maze. Right now, it doesn't look like there's much of the immediate family left."

"No." Julia was quiet as the memory of Trip's body lying face down on the carpet of his library popped into her head, as vivid as if it had just happened. She closed her eyes, took a breath, and opened them. "Tallulah hasn't lived here, or even in the states, for at least a decade."

"What about the brother? What's his name?"

"Satchell."

"Junior?"

"The fourth."

"Christ."

"Just be glad you're not having this conversation with Chappie. He can tell you about both sides of the sheets, whether true or not."

Mitch let his gaze wander to the window on the far side of the room. Julia watched him as he did his mental walkabout. It was as if he became a little more distant with each word out of her mouth.

The chasm between their worlds grew larger with each tidbit of knowledge. She wanted to shake him and shout that this was not her, but she knew in her heart the lady doth protest too much.

Finally, he stirred, glanced at her as if just remembering she was there and rose to his feet. "I think we need to pay Chappie another visit."

* * *

Chappie opened the door, a highball glass in one hand, and a decidedly unhappy look on his face.

"Come in, come in." He gestured as if he no longer had control over the vortex of events swirling around him. "The rest of your crew has already been and gone. Why don't I just give you a key? Hmm? Save us all a lot of trouble."

"Sorry about the inconvenience, Mr. Chapman, but

your butler has been missing for two days. With your car, I might add."

"I've told you, Deputy, Adoni does this on occasion. He finds living in a sleepy little place like Savannah a bit of a bore. He's accustomed to the more stimulating life of the European jet set."

They went into the morning parlor and he waved them toward the sofa. He lifted his glass in invitation but Mitch shook his head. "A little early for me."

"A little early for me too, if you must know, but all these histrionics about Adoni's whereabouts, the myriad loose ends for the exhibition, and that useless woman at the insurance agency would make a saint turn to drink." He had been pacing about the room as he spoke but after a gulp of his drink at the end of this diatribe, he sank into an armchair. "He couldn't have gone catting at a worse time." He sighed. "I blame it on Tallulah. He was part of her entourage in Milan and Paris. Her visit stirred all this up. Nothing more."

The look in Chappie's eyes belied his words. Mitch could see that he had doubts about the disappearance of his protégé. Did he fear Adoni had returned to his former life, or was there something else that made him so restless?

"Tell me about Aloyis Mercer."

The question, so out of the blue as it was, caused both Chappie and Julia to turn to him in unison.

Chappie sat up straighter, a spark in his eyes. "Aloyis Mercer Youngblood." He placed the highball glass on the side table. "Well, now Deputy, that is a story. One of our more flamboyant citizens if you discount Mame. She was married three times. Scandalous in and of itself for her time. The divorce from Higgs was the catapult that secured her reputation. Savannah is a southern town, after all." He crossed his legs and settled more comfortably in his chair. "What is it you wish to know, precisely?"

"I'm not sure. You mentioned her the other day and the name stuck in my head."

"Did I?"

"Something about art."

"Ah. Now I remember." He swung his leg back and forth and watched Mitch, a hint of a smile playing around his lips, a knowing look on his face. "Well, where to begin? Aloyis wanted badly to redeem herself in the eyes of the hoity-toity of her set. She decided that if she became a great connoisseur of art her behavior would transcend into that realm of the eccentric." He smiled at Julia. "But of course, she was no Mame, was she?"

"How did she go about this transformation?" Mitch asked.

"She married Mercer after the debacle with Higgs. She thought an attachment to such a cornerstone of Savannah society would do the trick. But she was impatient and when she was still being snubbed by polite society, she left her husband manning the home fires and went to Paris to hang out with the artistic set there. She followed in the footpath of other American ex-pats. She lived on the Left Bank near Luxembourg Gardens but she never quite made it into the coveted circle of Gertrude Stein. What allowed her into this lifestyle at all was her money. She had money, lots of money, so ex-patriots from all over the continent curried favor with her. She chose art over the literary world. Perhaps so as not to compete with Stein. As if she could."

"What does this have to do with anything?" Julia looked from Chappie to Mitch.

Chappie smiled. "Russian art. Am I right, Deputy?"

"It did occur to me when I was looking at your list, Julia. Why Russian art and why Savannah? What was the connection?" He smiled at her. "And after the genealogy lesson, I realized we needed to go back to the beginning. That would appear to be Aloyis Higgs Mercer Youngblood."

"She's been dead for nearly twenty years." Julia frowned. "How is that relevant?"

"She left her imprint on Savannah, and according to Chappie, on art. It occurred to me that perhaps she had a penchant for Russian art."

"Well, well, Deputy. Aren't you the shiny penny?" Chappie took a sip of his bourbon. "Russian art was near and dear to her heart. She donated a large part of her collection to the Louvre. There are even a few pieces in the Telfair Museum as well as several little boutique museums here and abroad."

"I see the thread, but don't see how it connects to the missing art we're looking for. Her collection was all over the place from realism to cubist. The stolen pieces tie together because of their historic period."

"And who, in Savannah, would know, from among all the Russian art in the area, where to find what the thieves were looking for? What was here, what was in the pipeline?" Mitch stood and retrieved his phone from his jacket pocket. "And how better to steal a valuable piece of art than when it was in transit, before it was under lock and key and tightly monitored."

Chappie and Julia spoke in unison, "Rocco."

"Aloyis Mercer Youngblood's protégé." Mitch stood staring at his phone. "Her word lifted him from the world of junk dealer to an authority on art. My guess would be that his discovery was of a Russian artist."

"Kazimir Malevich. One of the pioneers of geometric abstract art. He called his work suprematism. It was a huge innovation in art." Julia couldn't believe she had missed the connection. She was on the case because of her art background and yet she had missed the most glaring piece of evidence.

Mitch did a quick search on his phone then looked up at Chappie. "You're right. The back-of-the hand stuff is more enlightening." He extended his hand to Julia and they left Chappie happily ensconced in his chair, sipping his bourbon.

* * *

Rocco Sullivan's shop on Bull Street had that understated look that made the run of the mill tourist shy away from its door. There were no trinkets to be found within, no postcards to send home, and definitely no tee shirts or coffee mugs.

When Mitch and Julia entered the shop, a faint chime resounded through the space. Rocco Sullivan appeared from the rear of the establishment, impeccably dressed in a Savile Row suit. Mitch doubted there was a casual Friday dress code.

Rocco paused a beat when he saw them. Then he came forward. "Julia. How are you?"

"Hello, Rocco."

He glanced at Mitch and gave a little grunt. "I don't suppose you're here to shop, so what can I do for you?"

Mitch let Julia take the lead. He felt it would be less threatening. But then, maybe not. She had discovered a fraud among Rocco's dealings.

"I thought you could help." Julia said. "We're stumped as to what triggered a rash of art thefts in Savannah. It's not exactly the mecca of world class art, after all."

Rocco gestured with his hand for them to precede him toward the rear of the shop. In a back corner was an elegant sitting area arranged comfortably with what Mitch suspected were high-end antiques. He waited until Julia and Rocco were seated before taking a chair that created a triangle of the three of them.

Mitch let the silence draw out. Rocco seemed unperturbed by it. Finally, Julia spoke. "You're aware of the Fechin theft?"

"Certainly. It was in the news for weeks."

"Then, an exhibit of clothing belonging to King Christian IX went missing."

"I've heard rumors. Chappie has been adept at keeping it under wraps, but word gets out."

"And has word gotten out about Trip's painting of Peter the First by Serov?" Julia asked.

Rocco crossed his legs and adjusted the crease in his trousers. "Does this have anything to do with his death?"

"With his murder." Mitch leaned forward, his forearms resting on his thighs, and waited.

"I don't see how I can help you. It's true I went to Trip's house the night he died. I was there at his insistence. He was very much alive when I left. There's no way I can prove it but it's the truth."

Julia asked, "Is there anything else you can tell us about that visit? Sometimes something that seems quite ordinary can have unknown significance."

Rocco shook his head then stopped. "The phone rang.

I heard it just as Trip was closing the door behind me when I left."

He sat quietly until Julia again broke the silence. "Tell me about the Malevich and Aloyis."

"The Malevich? God, that's been ages ago. It hangs at the Telfair Museum, you know."

"Yes. I know."

Rocco smiled for the first time since they entered his establishment. "Of course, you do." He shook his head. "She made me with that painting. I found this dusty, ill cared for, peasant scene in an estate sale in one of those small Victorian houses to the south of the historic district. I looked up the signature but couldn't find anything on the artist. I thought I could clean it up and sell it for a few dollars."

"How did Aloyis come into the picture?" Mitch asked.

"I wrote her. This was in the days before any and everything you wanted to know could be found on the internet. There was something about the painting. I can't explain it, but I had it in the shop and every time I looked at it, I thought it was special." He lifted his hand dismissively. "I never thought I'd get an answer to my letter but a few days later a limousine pulled up to my shop door and out stepped Aloyis. And the rest, as they say, is history."

"Just like that," Mitch interjected. "Why do you think she came? You said you couldn't find anything about the artist."

"The signature. Malevich was known by his Russian name in art circles, but he always signed his work with his Polish name. There were a lot of Russians in Paris in the late twenties and early thirties. She realized who the artist was immediately."

"I don't understand. Was he Polish or was he Russian?"

"He was born of Polish parents but grew up under Russian domination due to the partitions. Essentially there was no longer a Poland at that point in history."

"Huh." Mitch sat back in the chair and gave this some thought then he stood, and Julia and Rocco followed suit. "You didn't broker the Fechin sale to the Peltiers, did you?"

"No. They found the painting while in Miami and dealt with the dealer there. They did call me and inquire about the reputation of the gallery. I assured them it was held in high esteem. Perhaps I did them a disservice with that advice."

"They contacted you before they made the purchase?"

"Yes. But don't think that gives me any more prior knowledge than half of Savannah. They couldn't stop talking about it at the reception they held for the opening of the Historic Homes Tour. They were thrilled to have found the perfect wedding gift for Fiona."

"Do you know Doug Heinz?"

"No."

"Also known as Viktor Letov."

"Again, Deputy, no."

Mitch gave a small nod of his head and turned toward the front of the shop. "Thanks for your time. You've been very helpful."

They walked down Bull Street toward Mitch's car. He held the passenger door open for Julia. "Did Rocco and Chappie know each other well?"

"Yes. Everyone who's involved in the arts or local history knows Chappie. I'm sure they've been on various boards together between the museum and other civic functions. And as I've explained, Savannah is a small town."

Julia slid onto the seat and watched Mitch as he rounded the front of the car and got behind the wheel. "Why?"

"Just trying to make the pieces fit."

They rode in silence for a couple of blocks.

"Why do you think they spared your Fechin?"

"Probably because very few people know about it."

"Why not?"

"After my great-grandfather died, Mame moved to the West Coast. She liked the warmth of the South, but she wanted to escape the smothering scrutiny. After a number of years, she ended up in Taos. She didn't return to Savannah until I was born."

"Where did she live when she came back?"

"Where I live now. She gave me the house in her will. The painting was a graduation gift several years before."

"How old was she when she died?"

"Ninety-eight."

"Has it always hung there in the office?"

"No. I had it in the safe during the renovations and only put it up once I moved in, three years ago."

"Uh huh."

"Where are we going?" Julia asked.

"The museum. I'd like to see this famous painting." He glanced over at her. "And I thought you were anxious to go there."

"I am."

"Care to tell me why?"

"The shipping crate. The one from the Fechin theft arrived in pristine condition, apparently. There were no indications it had been opened prior to arriving at the museum. The Peltiers had it shipped there so it could be evaluated before they sent it on to Fiona. All the packaging was as it should be, but the painting wasn't inside."

"How do you think that happened?"

"There are only two scenarios I can think of that would fit. The thief had an identical crate with all the seals, markings, and weight, which shipped instead. In that case the Fechin is still in Miami."

"And the other scenario?"

"Someone on this end managed to switch the original crate for an identical substitute somewhere along the route."

Mitch thought about that for a moment. "Either case suggests an inside accomplice."

"Exactly."

"Do you know that the packaging is still at the museum?"

Julia shook her head. "No. I can only hope. Chappie called the police when they opened the empty crate. They in turn called in the FBI since art theft is a federal crime. I have copies of all the photographs taken at the time, but I want to see the actual crate. Even with high-definition images, it just isn't the same as seeing it with your own eyes."

"Go to the original source when you can."

"Yes."

Chapter Twenty-Three

They parked on the street in front of the museum and went inside. The docent working the Sunday afternoon shift greeted them near the front door. She knew Julia and when she learned what they wanted, she glanced at her watch then led them into the rotunda gallery where the painting was on display.

It wasn't a large canvas. Mitch studied it, trying to see what could have made it touch Rocco Sullivan as it had. It was a peasant scene, the images more shapes than realistic figures.

"Is this suprematism? It looks like a child's painting.

"No. This is an earlier work. His most famous pieces are called Black Square and White on White."

"Odd names. What are they of?"

"A black square and a white square angled on a white canvas."

"You're kidding me, right?"

"No. The White on White is at the Museum of Modern Art in New York."

"And that kind of stuff is worth millions of dollars?"

"In this instance, yes."

"Christ." He continued to study the painting a few more minutes and shook his head. "Your great-grandmother got the better deal."

Julia laughed. "I agree."

The docent appeared in the doorway and told them it was time for the museum to close. Mitch showed his badge. "We're investigating the theft of the items for the Russian exhibition. Where would we find the original packaging materials?"

She looked from Mitch to Julia. "I suppose the custodian would know. He's waiting to lock up after I leave." She already had her purse on her arm and a sweater over her shoulders in preparation for closing up shop. "Let me secure the front entrance then I'll take you to him."

They found the custodian in a small vestibule beside a panel for the security system. He listened to what Julia and Mitch had to say and looked pointedly at his watch.

"We won't keep you long." Julia turned on her killer-watt smile and the custodian let the docent out the back door, locked it behind her, and turned with Mitch and Julia down a narrow hallway to the behind-the-scenes of the museum.

They went down a short flight of steps. At the bottom, a keypad opened a massive door with serious iron rods that fit into the door casing when closed. The room they entered was large with a high ceiling. The custodian turned on the overhead lights and showed them to an area to the right that contained a row of a dozen or more tall, cubicle-like walls. Each wall was covered with pieces of art front and back. They were so closely spaced there was barely room to walk between them. In the corner was a small built-out area not more than five by eight feet. Here, a table stood in the center with cubbyholes along the walls that held all kinds of packaging materials, some new, some obviously saved for reuse when needed.

The custodian didn't know exactly what they were looking for but told them it would be in this area somewhere if it was to be found at all. He would wait for them at the back entrance when they were finished. He had to make his rounds of the museum and be sure no hapless tourist had gotten overlooked and that all was secure.

"What's all this stuff?" Mitch asked Julia.

"It's the museum's inventory, things they don't have room to display."

"Why is there so much of it?"

"People donate things, sometimes something is offered for sale that they feel they can't pass up, and they need to be able to keep their exhibits fresh by changing things out occasionally. They also loan pieces to other museums for the same reason."

Mitch began poking around in the stacks of lumber and cardboard while Julia shifted through bubble wrap and acid-free paper tucked into cubbyholes along the wall behind the worktable.

The occasional noise reached their ears as they worked, a door closing somewhere overhead, the sound of water rushing in pipes briefly. These were the utterances of a building settling into the quiet of disuse at the end of a day. What sounded like a soft scrape appeared to come from somewhere in the room. Both Julia and Mitch stopped and listened.

"Does this place have rats?" Mitch finally asked.

"It had better not. Rats, damp, and harsh light are the nemesis of an art collection."

"I think this must be it," Mitch said as he pulled at a wooden crate penned within the materials leaning against the wall. "There're the initials MIA stamped in the wood. Looks like part of a logo and here's part of some kind of torn paper seal."

Julia abandoned her search and helped Mitch free the crate from the pile of other shipping discards. They lifted the container onto the table. She was scrambling around in her shoulder bag for the file folder with the photographs when the room was suddenly enveloped in darkness. The sound of the door to the room closing solidly and the sigh of the steel rods sailing home echoed around them.

Mitch spoke in a whisper. "Don't move and don't scream. I'm going to reach out and find your hand."

The darkness was smothering in its completeness. Even though he had prepared her for it, Julia jumped when he touched her arm. He made his way around the table, put his arm around her, and spoke close to her ear.

"We're going to squat and you're going to get under the table."

"Mitch…"

"I don't want to shoot you by accident, Julia. Do as I say."

He felt the tremble run through her.

"Is he in here?"

"I think not but I have to be sure. Stay put. Don't move until I give the all clear."

He felt a flood of relief wash through him when she complied without argument. Once he knew she was safe, he stood and let the darkness and silence settle around him. He rested a hand on the corner of the table and envisioned the space in his mind. When he felt he had his bearings, he set out on a path for the door, gun drawn.

He brushed one of the pieces of art on a half wall with his shoulder and stood in excruciating silence, listening for movement. Midway in his journey, his shoe connected with something he couldn't define. Finally, he felt the door, turned his back against it, lowered himself to a crouch, squinted his eyes, and flipped the light switch.

The room flooded with light. Mitch maintained his position until he was sure nothing moved within the room. Slowly he stood and began to crisscross the space, checking every nook and hiding spot. When he felt the room was secure, he returned to Julia and helped her emerge from beneath the table.

She threw her arms around him and pressed her face against his chest. He allowed himself the pleasure of her embrace for a brief moment then disentangled himself. "You're safe now."

"He was in here with us all along, wasn't he?" There was a slight tremor in her voice but then she seemed to regained control. "It's the Malevich, isn't it?"

"He was lying in wait so he could take it for his Russian collection."

"We have to stop him."

They moved in unison toward the door only to find what Mitch already knew. It was locked. He examined it to see if there was any hope of tripping the lock. It was as useless a prospect as breaking into Julia's shoe safe. He pulled out his phone and swore. No coverage. He hit the auto dial for backup anyway but there was nothing.

Julia read his expression. "It's the room. Whatever security precautions that went into its construction are blocking our reception." She ran back to the crating station and got her handbag. She took out her phone and found she had one bar. "Maybe I can get a text through."

Mitch rattled off a number as he looked around for something to use as a pry bar.

Julia typed in the text for help and pressed send. All they could do now was hope.

* * *

It's getting late and there's no sign of Julia. I have a certain level of confidence in Gerty but it isn't the same as my ability to keep her safe. Who am I kidding? I want to be in the know, in on the action. Curiosity Jones is probably a better name than Callahan. Maybe. Maybe not.

Julia thinks she's helping by leaving me behind. Her concern for my injury is admirable but wasted effort. The greater injury will be to my pride if I don't find a way to escape this confinement and catch the bad guy.

He's a sly one, this thief. Like a spider, he built a web meant to confuse and distract. But he's not as smart as he thinks he is. The bad guys rarely are. It has taken time and planning to pull all the strings of this grand scheme. And that's telling. We're looking for someone on the inside, someone with connections and the trust of all the insiders of Savannah's art scene. That narrows the field of players considerably.

I'm frustrated that Julia's concern has kept me at a distance from all the little telltale bits of behavior and snippets of information necessary for a quick resolution to this matter. All I can do is pace the floor and wait for her return.

But, wait. What's that I hear? I leap onto the window ledge and look below. It's Aunt Ethel arriving like a white knight in her iron horse. There's hope yet that I might save the day.

Her journey from the deep back seat of the large, and probably ancient, automobile to the sidewalk is a slow and painful process to watch. She doesn't have the agility and speed needed in a time of crisis. Her Ancient Charioteer is even less agile. I must be at the ready if we're to ride to the rescue, so to speak.

At last, she's at the door. I'm ready to streak through the opening the instant it opens but unfortunately, she's proven me wrong in my assessment of her frailty. Before I can slip past her, she has me caught up in her arms. The door closes firmly behind her. This is perhaps a talent of her stature, being as small as she is and so close to the ground. I can't deny that my injury plays a part in my failure to escape.

How, then, can I let her know we need to be on the case?

"Well, you. I see you've been up to your old tricks. Look at the mess in this room."

She bends down to collect the papers I have strewn about the floor in an effort to find the one clue that will break this case. Which might have been possible if I could read. But there is the image of a building on the shiny pamphlet with all the photos of art. Julia studied it intently and repeatedly. I feel it in my bones that this is where she has gone.

This is my chance, then. I must make Aunt Ethel see that we should be out the door and on our way to assist Julia.

Aunt Ethel may be old but she's sharp as a tack. If only I can show her the way. Ah. This is what I need. I separate the brochure

*from the scattered of papers on the floor before she can return it to
the file. I bat it around in the direction of the door of the apartment.*

"What are you up to?" *She follows after me and snatches up
the page.* "This is one of Julia's documents. It's not a play
toy."

*The insult almost distracts me from the urgency of my mission.
As she turns back toward the coffee table and the open file folder,
I begin to thread between her legs, obstructing her path, and pacing
back toward the door.*

*Aunt Ethel pauses and watches me as I walk a loop back and
forth from where she stands to the door and back again. She looks
down at the paper in her hands and begins to read it.* "The Russian
exhibit at the Telfair." *She turns the pamphlet over and reads
the back before she looks at me.* "Interested in Russian art, are
you?"

*"Yeow!" Is this human humor? Surely, Aunt Ethel is smarter
than that. Have I misjudged her?*

She stares at the page then looks up at me. "The museum."
"Yeow!"

"Well, all right then."

She picks me up and we head out the door.

*Our chariot awaits at the curb and if it were not for the need
to arrive at a destination that's unknown to me, I would be off in
a flash rather than wait for The Ancient to make the slow journey
around the automobile to facilitate our entry.*

*At last, we are ensconced in the rear seat of the car and after
much checking and rechecking the mirrors all around the vehicle, we
pull into the street and are off. I do hope our destination isn't too far
afield or I will have to take a nap before we arrive.*

* * *

Julia watched as Mitch struggled to find some crack or crevice around the doorframe large enough to give purchase to the claw of the hammer they found in the packaging room. She checked her phone once again. It had only been a few minutes but it seemed much longer. There was no way to tell if her message had gotten through as her phone now showed absolutely no bars.

Mitch stepped back to view the door from a different angle. "He knew what he was doing. This is someone who knows his way around the museum." He made a slow three-hundred-sixty-degree turn, surveying the high ceiling and the windowless room. "He wanted to detain us long enough to snatch the painting and escape."

He set off along the left-hand wall, checking behind large pottery urns, under tapestries hanging against the surface, tapping at the baseboard.

"What are you doing?"

"Looking for another door or some type conduit like a ventilation shaft. They had to have planned for air flow."

Julia moved to the right wall. "Do you think that was the plan all along? To collect the incoming art and at the last minute take the Malevich?"

"I don't know."

She threaded her way down an alleyway of partition walls toward the exterior wall. As she went, she glanced at the art hanging on either side of her. There was nothing but solid masonry to greet her at the end of the row. She had gone down three such alleyways when it struck her. "Mitch."

His voice came back to her from the far side of the room, hollow sounding because of the distance and the variety of objects between them. "Yeah?"

She turned and made her way toward the sound of his voice. "I know why he chose the storage room."

Mitch came from behind a huge statue of primitive man. "Yeah?"

"Come with me."

They returned to the rows and rows of framed artwork. "What do you see?"

"A bunch of paintings."

"Where do you hide something when you don't know how long you'll need to keep it hidden?"

Mitch rocked back on his heels and looked down first one alleyway and then another. "In plain sight."

"I think he came back here to collect the two paintings and the clothing. It was here all along. Mounted in the last place anyone would think to look."

"And convenient, too. He's known about the Malevich all along and then when he learned of Trip's latest painting and the Fechin, he decided the time was right. I think the clothing was just opportunistic."

Julia felt the hair stand on the back of her neck. "Someone in our inner circle has been lying in wait, possibly for years."

"It would seem so."

"And he's going to get away with it."

"Not on my watch."

"But there's nothing we can do if we can't get out of here." As soon as the words were out of Julia's mouth, they heard a mechanical grinding and the sliding of bolts.

They ran to the door and found the custodian standing there, though a bit wobbly on his feet. His head was bleeding but not excessively.

Mitch took him by the shoulders. "Are you all right?"

He nodded. "Go. The rotunda."

Julia glanced at her watch. They had been cooling their heels in the security vault for over fifteen minutes. Time enough for someone familiar with the facility to grab the Malevich and make a getaway. The only hope was that the need to transport more than one piece of art to his vehicle had slowed him enough for them to catch him.

The space on the wall of the rotunda where they had studied the painting only minutes before was blank.

"Which way?" Mitch had his phone out and had hit the speed dial.

"The docent locked the front door before she left. There's the back exit by the security panels and several others that lead out of rooms where special events are held. Delivery doors as well."

"Gerty…" After a moment's pause Mitch said, "Good," and closed the phone. "They're already on the way. Your message got through." He hesitated a moment longer. "Think, Julia. If you wanted to get in and out as inconspicuously as possible, what route would you take?"

"The West President Street exit. The landscaping creates a screen of sorts and the buildings on the other side sit back from the street and are only open on weekdays. At this late hour he'll have plenty of camouflage."

Even as she spoke, she ran out of the rotunda and through the museum in the direction of West President Street with Mitch hard on her heels.

* * *

"What's wrong with you, cat?" *Aunt Ethel tries to pull me into her lap, but I resist and continue to ride with my front paws on the top of the driver's seat, staring ahead at the total lack of traffic in front of us. Our blazing snail's pace is certainly no threat to automobile or pedestrian, but it might give me a heart attack. I realize I'm panting with anxiety.*

It apparently occurs to our Charioteer that the falling night is a call for him to activate the headlamps. In the process of doing so, we slow to a crawl that can hardly be called movement.

"Yeow!"

That seems to perk him up and as we turn a corner and travel a few feet, Aunt Ethel suddenly decides to become the navigator. "Turn here, Regis. Quick!"

There's nothing quick about Regis but he does in fact turn quickly, so quickly that he's unable to maintain control of the automobile and we glide to a not-quite-gentle halt against a dark gray Land Rover parked halfway onto the sidewalk. Not only have we hit the SUV square on, but we have trapped between the headlamps of our Rolls Royce, a tall, dark-haired man holding aloft a painting.

In the background is the wail of sirens and I know that what we are seeing is the great escape. I leap over the seat and paw at the door handle. Regis seems to come out of his stupor and opens the door. I scramble onto the hood of the Rolls Royce and stare down our culprit. Even if he weren't trapped between two bodies of British steel, he wouldn't get away from me.

Aunt Ethel gets out of the back seat, this time without waiting for the assistance of The Charioteer. "Chappie's butler. Well, I'll be."

Chapter Twenty-Four

Mitch and Julia raced along the pathway between the trees and shrubs on the south side of the museum to be greeted by the sight of Aunt Ethel, Regis, and Callahan staring at Adoni Bunin, trapped between two vehicles, when they arrived on the sidewalk of West President Street.

Cars with wailing sirens and blue lights skidded to a stop, blocking off both ends of West President Street and the surrounding streets. Armed deputies and FBI agents converged on the elderly couple and cat as they stood guard over the thief.

"Well," Aunt Ethel said, "I haven't had this much fun since I went skinny dipping with Jack Kennedy."

"Are you all right, Aunt Ethel?" Julia asked as she lifted Callahan from the hood of the Rolls Royce and came to stand by her.

"Of course, I'm all right."

"What are you doing here?"

"The cat," she said. "I went by to see you and he was pitching a fit among your papers. I figured out you had to be at the museum because he wouldn't leave the brochure alone. He was hell bent on getting to this address, so here we are."

"How did you know to stop Adoni?"

"Well, that just sort of happened. Regis' reflexes aren't what they used to be."

Gerty and another deputy stood at the ready, and when an FBI agent backed the Rolls Royce away from the trapped Adoni, she cuffed him and led him limping away to a waiting car.

Julia and the custodian verified that the Malevich was indeed the possession of the museum and handed it off to the authorities to take into evidence. She was also able to identify the Serov stolen from the Youngblood residence and that the third painting already in the back of the Land Rover was a Fechin. Presumably it was the one stolen while in transit to the Peltiers from the gallery in Miami.

There was no sign of the king's clothes.

Once the dust had settled, Julia got into the back seat of the Rolls Royce with Aunt Ethel. "Someone is going to drive you and Regis home."

"We can manage on our own."

"I know you can, but it will make all these law enforcement agents feel better if the man who almost committed vehicular manslaughter didn't get behind the wheel so soon after the incident."

"Very well."

Julia studied her and realized that for all her bravado, the excitement of the early evening had taken its toll. "Why did you come to visit?"

"I thought we'd plan a shopping excursion. You know, for the wedding."

"Maybe we should hold off on that for a while. He doesn't know about the wedding yet."

Aunt Ethel rested against the seatback and sighed. "Well, don't leave it too long. I'm not a spring chicken anymore and I can't shop like I used to."

Julia leaned over and kissed her on the cheek. "I won't."

* * *

Mitch closed the door to the interrogation room behind him to find Julia standing in the hallway waiting for him.

"I thought you'd be home by now." He said as he took her arm and led her toward the incident room.

"Really?"

He laughed. "No. You're much too nosey."

"I wouldn't call it being nosey. I'm investigating these thefts and it's my job to solve the mystery."

Mitch couldn't pass up such an opening. He looked down at her, his expression completely serious. "The butler in the library with a candlestick."

"Oh, you are a funny man."

"Yeah?" He grinned.

"Yeah." She kissed him.

Gerty cleared her throat as she closed the door rather more firmly than necessary. Julia and Mitch broke apart and stood staring at the murder board.

"Did he really act alone?"

"Yes and no." Mitch turned her toward the rear door of the office and handed off the file he had to Gerty as they passed her. "He saw Viktor when he came to Chappie's house to have the insurance forms signed, and he recognized him. After that he made it a point to befriend Debbie. Apparently, she likes dark, handsome men with accents."

"Viktor didn't have an accent."

"Okay, she likes dark, handsome men and the accent didn't hurt." Mitch opened the door to the back stairs, and they started down to the street below. "She was flattered and didn't realize Adoni was pumping her for details of Viktor's activities. He was biding his time, trying to decide when to turn Viktor over to his former associates."

"Why would he do that?"

"Money. Free, untraceable transport out of the country. He was going to be traveling with rather bulky stolen art pieces. You can't just buy a ticket on Delta."

"I see your point."

Mitch walked her to his car at the corner of the block. "From the time he became aware of it, the idea was to steal the Malevich. He knew the Russian billionaires were hungry for that type art and he wanted to get back to Europe and a lifestyle he enjoyed."

"Then why did he ever come to Savannah? He was riding on Tallulah's coattails, from what Chappie said. What made him ditch that in the first place?"

"He didn't ditch Tallulah. She ditched him. She picked him up at a high-end art gallery where he worked, but in return she expected exclusivity. That's not his strong suit."

"So, he latched onto Chappie."

"He thought Chappie would remain in Europe, allow

him to continue the lifestyle he'd grown accustomed to, and not make too much fuss over his errant ways."

"But Chappie came home."

"Yes." Mitch drove through the streets of the historic district in the quiet of a late Sunday night. "He learned about Trip's painting through an overheard conversation with Chappie. And the Peltiers made no secret of their purchase. He decided life would be much sweeter with more pocket money, so he broadened his scheme to include them. And you were right. He hid the items in the museum storage room until he was ready to make his move."

"How did he manage to move so freely past the museum's security?"

"He knew all the details of the facility. Chappie was the force behind the coming Russian exhibit, but Adoni was the grunt. Initially I thought Chappie might be behind it all. He seemed so intent on casting Adoni in the role of his everyman. Turns out it was the truth. Adoni handled everything, and everyone at the museum gave him access to what he needed because of it."

"What happened to the king's clothes?"

"They're still in the museum. Our arrival interrupted him in the process of moving the items from hiding to Chappie's Land Rover. He decided they weren't worth the risk. With the Malevich he had the real money items."

Julia sighed. "And two people are dead."

Mitch reached across and took her hand. "Yes. After Tallulah came to Savannah to meet with Ryder about the stolen jewelry, Adoni had to kill him. When she realized Adoni was in Savannah with Chappie, she accused him of being behind the robbery. If Ryder had learned of her suspicion, he would have started digging into his activities.

It would blow the whole plan."

There was a parking spot open directly in front of Julia's house. The street was empty of any traffic or pedestrians. No deputy or security guard loitered on the sidewalk. Mitch squeezed her hand.

"Come on, I'll see you to your door."

He handed her out of the car and took her keys from her when they reached the top step.

"Why did he kill Trip?"

"He came home from the party too early. Adoni was already in the house. From his time working in an art gallery in Milan and learning the ins and outs of the museum's security, he had no problem disarming Trip's system. He hid out, waiting for Rocco to leave and learned of the shooting from their conversation. He knew Chappie would be raising a stink about his whereabouts, and he couldn't afford to call attention to his absence on the evening Trip's painting was stolen. He misjudged Trip's actions. He thought Trip would turn in as soon as he let Rocco out the front door. Instead, he returned to the library and caught Adoni in the act. Adoni took the heavy brass candlestick from the fireplace mantle and struck him twice. He couldn't afford to let him live."

Julia shivered and Mitch put his arms around her. "This is not the stuff of bedtime stories. Let's leave it for now." He unlocked her front door and ushered her into the foyer. He did a quick scan of the street before locking up behind them, then allowed his gaze to travel around the entryway.

"You're not helping matters," Julia said. "The danger is over. Stop looking in the shadows."

"Habit of the profession, I'm afraid. Sorry."

They went upstairs and he unlocked the apartment

door. Julia stepped inside as he hovered on the threshold.

"What made Aunt Ethel decide to visit this afternoon?"

"She wanted to go shopping." Julia smiled and the light returned to her eyes. "For shoes."

"Shoes. Of course." He grinned. "Where?"

"Milan."

"Milan, Italy?"

"They have the finest Italian leather."

"And you're a woman in need of a pair of shoes."

"I am. I need a pair of shoes to wear to a wedding."

"Am I invited to this wedding?"

"There can't be a wedding if you're not there."

He stood staring down into her upturned face. His heart had been lost the first time he laid eyes on her. He thought, what the hell. If the Prince of Monaco could take on Grace Kelly, a U.S. Marshals' deputy could marry a Southern belle, crazy relatives, shoes, and all. "Where's the cat?"

"He went home with Aunt Ethel. She lured him with promises of grilled cheese sandwiches before Dax comes to claim him tomorrow."

"No chaperone?"

She smiled and shook her head.

With that, Mitch stepped across the threshold and closed the door.

Thank you for taking the time to read *Callahan's Savannah Caper*. If you enjoyed it, please consider telling your friends or posting a short review. Word of mouth is an author's best friend and is much appreciated.
Thank you!

Rebecca

An avid reader since the bookmobile began coming to their farm when she was a child, Rebecca Barrett now happily lives in the lovely village of Fairhope, Alabama, situated on Mobile Bay, where she finds inspiration all around her.

Visit her website at www.rebeccabarrett.com
Email Rebecca: barrett.author@gmail.com

* * *

**Cat Callahan Mysteries by Rebecca Barrett and
Susan Yawn Tanner:**
Callahan on the Case
Callahan and the Horses of Hope
Callahan's Savannah Caper
Callahan Goes Rodeo
Callahan and the Spy
Callahan in Action

Callahan's Christmas Feast (short story)
A Callahan Christmas (short story)